THE
ALPHA'S
SALVATION

by

MARLOWE ROY

Content Advisory
(contains spoilers)

This is a work of omegaverse fiction. It contains themes of suicide, post-traumatic stress, domestic violence, sexual violence, and abduction.
It also contains mature language and explicit sexual content.

Reader discretion is advised.

Table of Contents

CHAPTER 1

Kess

"The g-gar… the garbage truck?" Mills peeked at Kess over the top of his book, checking his pronunciation. Kess gave him an encouraging nod to continue. "The garbage truck co… collected every Tuesday—"

"What's a garbage truck?" Ani interrupted.

Kess sighed and pointed at the picture accompanying the text. "I think," she said as the younger students crowded closer to see the big green vehicle, "before TheEnd, these trucks would drive around and collect things people no longer wanted."

"What kinds of things?"

"Like food?"

"No one would throw away food, stupid."

"None of that, Jak." She arched a brow at her surly eight-year-old pupil, satisfied as he lowered an admonished chin toward his chest. With an internal sigh, Kess turned her attention back to the book, silently lamenting—once again—the limitations of the schoolhouse materials. "I don't believe I've ever seen a garbage truck myself."

Despite their initial suggestion she use only the Christian Bible to teach, she'd convinced the village parents to let her make use of everything she had available. Unfortunately, everything consisted of a mishmash of books and magazines scavenged decades before, all of it tattered, yellowing, missing pages, and filled with references to a way of life that hadn't existed for over a hundred years. Some days, it seemed, she spent her school hours trying to explain things she didn't even understand to the two dozen big-eyed children entrusted to her.

Certainly no one was making new books in the AfterEnd. No one was making anything new at all, except for babies. Babies never stopped coming.

At least for some people.

Shadows flickered in the doorway of the ramshackle schoolroom, letting her know the parents had come to collect their kids. Where had the day gone? Her stomach growled an answer, and she soothed her palm against the aching organ, ever-reminded of her dependence on the village's goodwill for her survival. She provided lessons, and in exchange, the families shared their food, albeit inconsistently.

In a few weeks, the blossoming spring weather might provide some mushrooms and green onions to gather, but for now, the village relied on their winter stores—mostly meat and whatever grain remained. Hopefully, someone would leave something today, as her larder was as empty as her belly.

More than once she'd fantasized about an existence less reliant on others, but given what she'd escaped, she took what she could get.

Shaking off the thought, Kess dropped her hand from her complaining stomach. "Let's stop there for today."

At her dismissal, the children exploded in a flurry of after-school excitement. Smiling at their lively chatter, she closed the book about the mythical garbage truck, sparing a wonder for where they had all gone in the AfterEnd. In her travels, she'd seen decaying cars aplenty littering the landscape, but she couldn't recall ever seeing an abandoned garbage truck anywhere.

"Miz Kess," a deep, chilling voice intruded, his enormous, yet familiar silhouette engulfing hers. "I have some food for you."

Heart kicking in her chest, Kess gathered up the meager school supplies, disguising her shaking hands from the village's only Alpha.

Heck was an Alpha, but a new one. His Alpha senses still developing, he hadn't recognized her Omega scent in any conscious way, yet had begun to linger after class and routinely brought her more than a usual payment of food.

The behavior terrified her.

When she'd joined the village three years past, she'd harbored a secret fondness for the scrawny, lanky boy who reminded her of her long-lost younger brother. She'd been as shocked as anyone when, six months ago, seventeen-year-old Heck began his Alpha transformation by shooting up six inches in height and packing on muscle, despite the winter food austerity. In retrospect, had her own innate Omega recognized his latent Alpha and manifested her fondness for him? She'd never know.

Omegas birthed Alphas sired by other Alphas, but Alphas were also sometimes randomly produced by Beta humans. Heck was one of these. His full transition would take years, his body changing and his senses heightening and honing. As he changed, Beta society would only tolerate him for a short while.

It wasn't even their fault. It was the genetics, the change in the human code that had happened at TheEnd to reorganize the world into Beta humans, Alphas, and Omegas. People he grew up with would instinctively cower before him and resent him because of it. In this village, she'd already heard mutterings suggesting the Alpha mutation was a curse, or even a "mark of Cain."

Eventually, as happened with all Alphas, he would leave and find his way to live among his Alpha brothers. She'd seen the anxiety lining his parents' faces when they looked at him, as if hoping he would stay in the village and not become an Alpha like *those* Alphas.

Kess hoped for the opposite—that he'd leave the village before realizing the full truth of her Omega nature, or even worse, his presence kicked her into a Heat. If she could keep her distance, she could remain hidden, an Omega among the Betas.

Having fought and bled for her freedom, now secrecy preserved her independence. She had belonged to an Alpha once, and she'd vowed she would never again.

Despite this, deep in her heart, Kess ached for Heck as much as she feared him. Ripped from her home and brought west as a teen, she knew what it was to leave your family and everything you knew, never to return. Yet her bitterness reminded her that at least Alphas claimed some amount of agency in their new lives. An Omega's fate remained a far more uncertain thing.

Setting the garbage truck book aside, Kess steeled herself for the interaction, schooling her expression into pleasant blandness. "You already brought me food this week."

He lifted a massive shoulder and grinned. "You have to eat more than once a week, don't you?"

"Other people bring me food." She edged past him to help a younger student with his jacket. Not wanting to encourage Heck, she avoided even a casual brush of her skin against his.

"Not enough," he groused under his breath. He stepped closer, grazing her arm as she fussed with the child's zipper and injecting apprehension straight into her blood. "I know for a fact half these kids never bring you nothing."

Kess tapped the jacketed child on the head and shuffled them to the door, putting as much distance between herself and the Alpha as she could.

When she turned, only she and Heck remained in the cleared schoolroom. "Everyone struggles to eat, Heck. I don't want children going hungry on my account."

He shoved a cloth-wrapped bundle at her. "Here. There's some dried meat and a few boiled eggs. And an onion, but you'll need to cook it."

Her stomach answered, announcing her hunger and bringing an expression of smug satisfaction to his face. "An egg sounds really good," she admitted, accepting the bundle. "Thank you. And please thank your parents for me too."

Hope buoyed his eyebrows. "You coming to the fire tonight?"

Once a week, the entire village came together to build a bonfire and socialize. Kess dreaded fire night almost as much as she dreaded the Sunday sermons, only those she didn't dare skip. But on fire night, she preferred to stay in her small cabin and re-read one of her precious few books. Right now, she was working her way through the near-incomprehensible *Doctor Zhivago* a trader had left last year. On her fifth read-through, she almost grasped the plot, although the book depicted a time two hundred years before in a place that might not exist anymore.

So many places had been destroyed in TheEnd. Places she could only visit through fading, water-warped books. Places that might be pure fiction, overlaying a past as grim and brutal as her present. She'd never know, but she wanted to believe the truth lay between the lines of the stories, that there had been a time of trains, glistening ballrooms, and more than two sets of clothing. She needed it to be true—depended upon it for hope, in fact. If that had been true then, maybe it could be true again.

"I don't know." She raked a hand through her greasy curls. "I need to… wash my hair."

His face folded in disappointment. "Well, okay. You can dry it by the fire… if you want to."

"We'll see." She infused her answer with as much finality as she could, hoisting the bundle in her fist. "Thanks again for the food."

Not waiting for his response, she set the food aside and devoted herself to neatening the room. His presence pulsed at her back, an almost palpable sensation of Alphaness breathing down her neck and encroaching on her senses.

She hated it. She didn't want it.

But she loved it.

No. She didn't love it. That deep, sick part of her, the Omega loved it. Craved it.

After a small eternity, Heck's heavy footsteps pounded out the door, his burgeoning Alpha presence retreating in his wake. A sweat broke out on her forehead, and terror stiffened her muscles. *Oh fuck. Oh no.*

No, no, no.

He couldn't provoke a Heat, could he? He wasn't even fully developed, not to mention she hadn't had a Heat in five years. Could she even still have them? Beta women had a menopause—did Omegas? Maybe. She'd never known an Omega in her forties to ask.

No, this couldn't be a Heat. The room had warmed as the sun came out, and Kess still wore her thick winter coat. Plus Heck made her nervous. She needed to stay away from him, maybe even talk to his parents about ceasing his schooling. He'd be hurt, and her inner Omega cringed at upsetting an Alpha, but his ongoing development was a growing risk. How long till he left to find a Pack? If not soon, she'd need to run.

Again.

Although five years in the past, the memories of her harrowing journey stalked her every waking moment. Sometimes Kess lay awake at night and marveled at how she'd ever snuck away from Brock's Alpha Pack.

Knowing her Omega scent would broadcast her presence to any Alpha in the vicinity, she had taken no chances. In preparation, she'd clipped her hair short and shaved off all her body hair, then burned the evidence. Trudging north for weeks, every night, no matter how tired, she'd aggressively washed her body of all traces of sweat. She'd scrubbed under her arms and between her legs with leaves and sand until her skin oozed blood. Then she'd dressed, piling Brock's clothes on top of her own, all to conceal her aroma and pass unnoticed and undisturbed.

But the fact she'd faked a mourning period probably accounted for her unimpeded escape more than anything. No one suspected she had gone until she was far away. Maybe they thought she'd disappeared to kill herself.

Maybe they just didn't care to come after her.

That wasn't the case, though; she knew it in her soul. An Omega would've never been allowed to casually stroll away from the Pack. No matter how much of an object of disdain they found her, Omegas were too rare. No amount of pity would've stopped the more determined Alphas from making a play for her, Brock's friends or no. She'd heard the rumblings not even a week after Brock's death and had felt their sticky gazes on her as the Pack gathered to burn his body.

No one would touch her until the Alpha of Alphas permitted, but she knew it was only a matter of time until he caved to their demands and she found herself cornered. Being claimed by another Alpha would've been the best-case scenario. The worst—being held down and fucked by half the Pack—was too horrible to consider. Her stomach clenched again, not from hunger, but from the old fear spiking through her.

As long as she remained in this village with a burgeoning Alpha in her midst, she tempted fate. Heck's nature would strengthen, and hers would answer. And she'd be claimed and locked up.

With a shuddering sigh, Kess gulped her panic down. It didn't fill her empty belly, but she needed to think this through with a clear mind. Preferably on a full, or at least fuller, stomach.

Class tidied, she left the schoolroom and lifted the lid on the donation bin outside, where families would leave her payment when they had it.

Empty.

Clutching Heck's offering tight, she made a beeline for her small shack on the edge of the village. This food needed to last at least another few days.

CHAPTER 2

Hunter

Goddammit.

He'd been ready to call it quits for the night when Sloan spotted smoke tendrils snaking into the sky. They'd been riding south for two days without any sign of Betas, and Hunter was ready to turn around and head home.

Maps being a thing of the past, no one knew the exact boundaries between the Alpha lands and the Beta territories, but tribal lines were clear. Alphas lived in Packs, along with their Omega mates, when they had them. Betas, both male and female, stayed away, carving out quiet lives for themselves in the wilderness. While some of the more feral Alpha Packs bullied and terrorized the smaller, weaker Betas, Alphas mostly kept to themselves, impinging on Beta lands only for peaceful trading and, occasionally, some less-than-peaceful Omega raids. His Pack claimed lands north of these, and he was old enough to remember the area used to be known as British Columbia. That made him... too fucking old.

Bored after months of winter and impatient for the thaw, his Pack had lobbied for weeks for a trip to the Beta lands south of them. They'd presented any number of excuses: things they wanted to trade for, items they wanted to salvage, seeds they wanted to acquire. But he knew the truth. They were horny. Every last one of them, from the youngest pup, Alek, to his Second Alpha, Colt—they all reeked of it. If Hunter could smell himself, he probably did as well.

But he was used to it. One didn't live for a hundred years as a transformed Alpha in the AfterEnd without withstanding periods of long, hard horniness. He could recall every last pussy he'd ravaged in that time, and it wasn't nearly enough. Once, he'd counted it up and figured out that he'd fucked more women in his thirty years before TheEnd than in his hundred in the AfterEnd.

That made sense, as much of the population had died off, and encounters with anyone had become few and far between. So many had died. Millions, probably billions. There was no way to count. And then there were the changes. The very nature of humanity had mutated and perverted before his very eyes.

A constellation of manmade and natural disasters had changed the world in a matter of months. First came the nuclear attacks—either due to terrorists or pure stupidity, no one was ever sure. In his darkest moments, he suspected some moron somewhere had opened an email promising a peek at some actress' tits, and that had set the end of the world in motion. However it had happened, it had only taken one missile launch to trigger retaliations that brought the world damn close to "mutually assured destruction." Cities, power grids, food and fuel depots targeted. One of the last news reports Hunter had ever heard said the city of Cincinnati had been annihilated, and seriously, who the fuck ever cared about Cincinnati? Didn't matter. Blasted to smithereens along with so many others, all in a period of a week.

Then, like a Biblical prophecy, came the earthquakes, the floods, the fires, and the disease.

And the radiation. From what he guessed, the radiation had activated some kind of dormant genetic variant in a fraction of the survivors. No labs existed for scientists to explain or investigate it. Fuck, there weren't any fucking *scientists* anymore. He'd watched people die while his body grew stronger, taller, faster, like a superhero origin story from those inescapable comic-book movies. Only he was no hero—he was pure monster. All anyone knew was that the world had changed overnight, and what humanity remained had become this sick fucking world of Alphas, Omegas, and Betas. The strong and the weak, a hundred years later, eking out an existence as best they could.

And Hunt lived on.

The landscape shifting from the barren wasteland of a nuclear winter to early regrowth and the gradual return of vegetation confirmed the blurred passage of time. Thirty years old when TheEnd came, he estimated a hundred years had passed since, give or take five. His "superior" genetics had not only changed his body, but slowed his aging to a snail's pace. One hundred and thirty years old, and he looked no more than fifty to his own eyes. Fucked up, it was.

He was sick of it. Of all of it. That was probably why he'd relented to his Pack's desperate pleas for the trading adventure. Not out of horniness, but out of boredom, and a secret reason he barely admitted to himself.

Hunt wanted to die. He'd had enough of life in the AfterEnd. He hated that he called it that, hated that he *thought* of it like that. But he hated his life most of all, and before the end of this trip, he'd fucking end it.

Alphas could die. It didn't happen often, but it happened. Usually accidents took them, due to their own stupidity or brazenness, or sometimes they died in battles with other Alphas that went too far. He'd seen bears pick off a few in his time as well. He'd never seen an Alpha die of old age, but he'd never met one as old as himself. He figured if he stabbed himself in the heart, then pitched himself over a cliff into the ocean, he'd both bleed out and drown, and maybe bust his skull on some rocks for good measure.

And that would be that. His own personal end. The thought of it filled him with peace like nothing else. He hadn't had a choice in surviving TheEnd. Hadn't had a choice in transforming into an Alpha. Hell, he hadn't really had a choice in becoming leader of this Pack. But this... this was solely his choice, and he'd made it.

In preparation, he'd left the territory in the hands of some trusted Alphas, content they'd protect their community. After the initial decades of devastation, witnessing violence and exploitation on his travels, Hunt and a small Pack organized and claimed their lands twenty years prior. They named it Morris Hill in honor of his brother, ran Betas (and the more deplorable Alphas) off, and set about creating a safe place for their rapidly growing families. It wasn't perfect, but he'd tried.

Yet it wasn't enough. A month ago, he'd said a silent goodbye to Morris Hill and all the mixed feelings he had about the place. Sure, they'd kept some Omegas and their pups safe, but the laughter and warm families only reminded him of his failures and all he'd lost.

The Pack had been traveling south for a month and were about to turn back and take a return route along the coast. Keeping with his plan, he'd scout for a location to end this nightmare existence. Colt would guide the Pack home without him. Guilt twisted his guts for abandoning Colt without warning, but he couldn't risk interference. Colt, the most honorable Alpha Hunt had ever known, would do everything in his power to prevent Hunt from carrying out his plan. For that reason, trusted Second or not, Colt couldn't know.

None the wiser to his intentions, from his Pack's perspective, it had been a successful trip. Along the way, they'd traded with some small Beta villages. His Pack had managed to fuck some willing Beta women here and there, and they'd even sniffed out a few Omegas and two new Alpha pups. The Omegas had been escorted back to their territory to get them settled in their new lives. He'd learned in his years as Alpha of Alphas that Omegas needed quick integration into the Pack, preferably with a bonded Alpha. An unclaimed Omega only caused trouble.

Fucking Omegas. From an evolutionary standpoint, he didn't get it. The Alpha mutation that had rendered him larger, stronger, faster, and better able to survive in the post-apocalyptic world, he could understand. But the Omegas... their primary adaptation seemed to be increased sex appeal and mind-bending fertility. Hunter could only speculate as to the Beta maternal mortality rate in the AfterEnd, but of the Omegas he'd seen, not one had suffered birth complications anywhere near what he would anticipate for a society blasted back to pre-modernity. With his own eyes, he'd seen Omegas birth a pup a year for ten-plus years and suffer no ill health effects. In fact, they seemed to get healthier with each one, even while pushing out giant Alpha babies that averaged nine or ten pounds.

Maybe it made sense. If humans were to survive, they needed to reproduce faster, and Omegas seemed to be the key to that. Whereas Betas could randomly pop out Alphas and Omegas among their Beta babies, Alpha-Omega pairs birthed only Alpha and Omega pups. If Omega birth rates surpassed Beta, then eventually Betas would go the way of the Neanderthal, out-survived by their better-adapted cousins.

Problem was, Omegas remained rare. Sure, they were sweet and soft, and their bodies could take an Alpha cock better than any Beta could hope to in her wildest dreams, but the Omega mutation made them unstable. As much as Alphas could be reckless and stupid, he'd seen enough Omegas go absolutely batshit to avoid the whole business. The ones who were strong did all right and formed bonds he'd envied once upon a time. But the weak-minded ones sometimes couldn't handle their powerful Heats. They'd either go so deep into it they would refuse sustenance and basically fuck themselves to death despite their Alpha's best efforts, or they'd fight against the Heat and end up near-psychotic from refusing to fuck.

He could only speculate, but perhaps the instability accounted for their relative scarcity. If a certain percentage died during their early Heat cycles, then they died young before reproducing. Perhaps over time, the stronger Omegas who bonded would remedy the situation with their impressive fecundity.

Omegas were the only thing any Alpha wanted, and the last thing they should want. They both craved and ruined the other.

What a mess.

If he tried, he could conjure up memories of women from before TheEnd. Smart, sophisticated women who painted their faces with makeup and made coy conversation called flirting. They were as far from this world as Venus was from Earth. Those women were all dead. Or, if they'd become Omegas, maybe they'd lived too long like him, long enough that all their sophistication and grace would've been rubbed away, or raped out of them by the harsh reality of the AfterEnd. It bothered him.

"The village is up ahead, Alpha," Colt said, interrupting his brooding.

Hunt blinked a few times to clear his thoughts. He'd have been embarrassed, except one—an Alpha never felt embarrassed about anything, and two—Colt knew he was a broody bastard.

Hunt cast a brief glance at the horizon. The sun had fallen in the time it had taken them to track the smoke, and darkness descending before his eyes. A pack of a dozen

Alphas on horseback riding into their village would scare the living shit out of those Betas.

"Signal the others," Hunt said. "Let's dismount and walk in, or it'll be a fucking panicked disaster."

"Yes, Alpha." Colt turned his horse to pass the word along the line. The Alphas obeyed—his Pack knew their fucking places, at least—and they made their way toward the village.

From half a mile away, he could smell their acrid Beta stench, along with the smell of roasting meat—rabbit, and maybe some squirrel. He grimaced. This must be a pretty fucking hard-up village to be eating scrawny spring squirrels. They wouldn't find shit here to trade.

The sharp kick of high-proof alcohol hit his nose on the next breath.

Okay, maybe there'd be *something* to trade.

"Ho!" he called out, emerging from the tree line into the village clearing. A quick look around confirmed it was, indeed, a fucking shithole. Poorly constructed shelters were scattered around the central pit, where a roaring bonfire sent up the smoke signal they'd seen. Off to the side, they'd erected three giant crosses. He stifled an automatic eye roll. So it was one of those villages.

His brain calculated about fifty pairs of Beta eyes staring back at him from the village, all silent and terrified, and growing more so as the full dozen of his beastly Pack became visible in the firelight.

A Beta male separated from the crowd, and Hunt couldn't hold back a smirk. Every village had one, some sort of jackass, self-appointed representative. Who did he fancy himself? The preacher? The mayor? Whoever he was, hopefully this one wouldn't be some supercilious prick who would stupidly posture and try some shit with an Alpha. Betas sometimes forgot why they were Betas. Especially out here in the wilderness of the northwest, where an Alpha Pack may not have come around for years.

Behind him, Hunt caught sight of a young Alpha pup, his pants and shirtsleeves rendered comically short from rapid growth. Black hair stuck out at odd angles around his head. With his long legs, he quickly caught up and took his place next to the Beta who resembled him. His father, then. The Alpha pup's eyes were round and unblinking, but his jaw was set with determination to face a pack of Alphas and not look like a fucking pussy.

Hunt liked the look of him. They'd leave with another member in their Pack.

"Alpha," the pup said, instinctively craning his neck in deference. "Welcome to our village."

Hunt acknowledged the respect with a brisk, approving nod, and the pup visibly relaxed.

"We don't have anything of value here," the Beta stammered. "Our food stores are depleted, and—"

"Did I say anything to you, Beta?" Hunt barked. He cut the Beta a look of bored disdain. "Keep your fucking mouth shut while I talk to the pup here." He refocused on the pup. "My Pack and I have been traveling, trading with Betas. We aren't interested in *taking* anything from you, but I'm sure some of these Alphas would be happy to trade for a bit of that grain alcohol you have on your breath. You can tell your village we mean them no harm, women or otherwise. I don't hold with rape in any form, but if there are some willing bedmates, my Pack would like to meet them, I'm sure."

Ignoring the Beta's choked-off protest, he flashed a feral grin over his shoulder, mostly to assure his Pack he was looking out for their best interests. The horny fuckers would definitely consider their dicks as their "best interests."

"Thank you, Alpha," the pup said. "I'm sure we can find some more alcohol. There's a stream that runs behind the village; you can water your horses and camp there, if you like." His eyes widened at inadvertently telling a superior Alpha what to do. "Or wherever you want to camp, Alpha, I—"

Hunt cut him off. "Yeah, we'll do that." He knew what the kid meant. No need to be more of an asshole than necessary. Hunt handed his reins to Sloan. "Take the horses to the water and get the camp set up." He slapped a palm on the pup's Alpha-scrawny shoulder. "I'm going to have a chat with our new Pack member here."

CHAPTER 3

Kess

Kess kept her fire small in her cobbled-together hut. Its ventilation wasn't sufficient to manage the smoke and not choke her to death. Plus, she'd gone ahead and washed her hair and didn't want it to smell like smoke. But who was she kidding, really? Her entire life, her hair had smelled like smoke, and the aloe she smoothed on it to ease the tangles and tame her tight curls. Or at least try, anyway. It had grown back in the five years since she'd left Brock's Pack, and now it dusted the tops of her shoulders when dry. When wet and combed out, it extended almost to the tips of her breasts. She worked the comb gently through the tangles and breathed in the solitude.

The sounds of the bonfire and the villagers passed through her walls, but they were only a rumble in the back of her mind. After a small meal of one of the eggs and half the meat Heck brought her, she'd scavenged for some bitter watercress down by the creek to round out her dinner. The rest would wait for tomorrow. She hated living day to day like this, but it beat the alternative.

When she'd been mated to Brock, he provided for her needs, but otherwise kept her isolated from the rest of the Pack. Occasionally she'd get to see the other Omegas, but not enough to feel they were her friends. Brock had thought if she stayed at home and "nested," she'd be more likely to conceive and give him the litter he wanted. Cycle after cycle, they tried for children, but one never took hold. With no pregnancy to interrupt them, in her fifteen years with Brock, she'd endured more Heat cycles than any other Omega. Maybe that was the reason she hadn't had one in so long. Maybe her body had simply tired of it. She could hope, at least.

Despite it all, she was thankful she'd never conceived. Escape would never have been possible if she'd had pups to slow her down. And she'd heard whispered horror stories of Alphas killing the pups of their Omega's prior mate if they were senseless enough in a Rut. She shuddered at the thought.

So while Brock spent time tussling and hunting with his brothers, she spent her days in utter and complete boredom, so much so she'd taught herself to weave baskets from dried grass and reeds to pass the time. Now on the other side of her hut, a large stack of baskets, small and large, piled next to the depleted basket where she kept her gathered materials. She'd run out of basket-making materials a month ago. Hence *Doctor Zhivago*.

A knock sounded at her door, and terror stuffed her throat. She sniffed the air, searching for Heck's salty Alpha smell. If he cornered her in her hut...

She'd hidden a knife under her pillow, but she wasn't stupid enough to think she could defend herself against even an emerging Alpha pup. But she might slow him down enough to run. If she ran to his parents' hut, maybe they'd intervene before he mounted her. Kess stilled her breathing, assuring herself she scented no Alpha on the wind. She took an additional clear, calming breath.

She lived in fear of Heck. He was young and sweet, sure, but his presence posed a serious danger to her. More so with each passing day. Maybe it was time for her to leave this village and find another.

"Miz Kess," a little voice said. "Are you there?"

Kess laid a hand over her relief-flooded heart. "Yes, I'm here, Ani."

Rushing to open the door, her youngest pupil stood outside her hut, cheeks pinked and grinning ear to ear. She thrust a small pouch at Kess. "These are for you. It's nuts!"

Squatting to the child's level, Kess accepted the pouch, cupping Ani's cheek. She hadn't been totally forgotten by the village today. She smiled. "What kind of nuts? Do you know?"

"Brown ones."

"Mmm, sounds delicious." Kess surveyed the area beyond her door, the frosty air seeping in and chilling her beyond the protection of her modest fire. Night had come in the time she'd been tending to her hair, and the dark had thickened so she could barely see five feet away. "Ani, did you come here by yourself?"

The six-year-old grinned even bigger. "Yes! All by myself!" Her grin wilted into a sheepish look. "Mama sent those nuts for you, but I forgot to give them to you at school, so I brought them so Mama wouldn't be mad."

"I see. Well... I'd better walk you back to the fire before your mama realizes you're missing. She'll be worried, don't you think?" Kess rose from her crouch and pushed her sleeves into her coat, resigned to make an appearance at the bonfire. Hopefully, once she dropped Ani off with her mom, she'd sneak back to her warm, safe hut. As a final thought, Kess grabbed her knit cap, but hesitated to plop it on top of her still-drying hair.

"Can I wear your hat, Miz Kess? Please? Please?" Ani jumped up and down. The hat was rainbow-colored, and all the kids loved it. Kess had traded for it a few years back and secretly loved it even more than the kids did. The bright colors sang to her soul, especially in a world as grim as theirs could be.

She gave Ani a stern look. "Just until we get you to your mom, then I have to take it back, okay?"

"Yes! I'll give it right back!" Ani's grabby little fingers snatched it, and she had it on her head in two seconds, grinning wildly as it fell over her eyes.

"Silly." Kess folded it up to restore the youngster's vision. "You can't walk around a fire not looking where you're going." She took Ani's hand in her own and shut her door. "C'mon, let's go."

Kess' hut was on the outskirts of the village, farthest from the creek. When she'd arrived there three years ago, it had been the only open dwelling, and she had moved in with extreme gratitude. After travelling for two years, constantly on the run, she'd been so thankful to be welcomed and accepted, she would've slept anywhere they allowed her. The adults in the village had assured her—when she'd gradually, carefully, casually worked her way around to the subject—that no Alphas had been spotted here in years. No one was quite sure why, but she didn't question it. Several years with no Alpha contact sounded perfect.

Flickering firelight danced across the other dwellings, and the voices increased in volume as they got closer. Kess' skin tightened, her muscles hiccupping to a stop and refusing to move. She scanned the woods, alert for signs of movement in the shadows. Coyotes and wolves ranged in this area, and a small child would be a tasty snack to carry off.

Ani pulled at her hand. "C'mon, Miz Kess, I wanna show Mama your hat."

With another sweep, Kess took a stuttering step forward, her body protesting every inch. Icy fear gripped her, and her instincts screamed at her to *go back, go back*! If not for the child, she would've bolted straight home. Instinct had saved her enough times that she knew to heed her internal alarms.

But she couldn't leave Ani alone in the dark. The child was dragging her along, anyway. At the edge of the clearing, Kess' eyes blinked to accommodate the fire's brightness. The village had really gone in for it tonight. Flames shot up into the sky, almost to the top of the trees, and the voices seemed louder and more menacing than usual. Foreboding solidified in her belly like a block of ice. What the hell was going on?

"Mama! Mama!" Ani yelled, darting away to where her parents sat poking at potatoes in the fire. "Miz Kess let me wear her hat!"

Kess scanned the crowd, and the wind shifted the moment her gaze landed on a massive, silvering Alpha talking to Heck. Sharp, potent Alpha scent—no, *several* Alpha scents—shot up her nose, and her hands trembled at her sides.

They were here. She couldn't tell how many, but more than a few.

A Pack had found her.

Kess spun on her heel and willed her feet to walk as fast as they could without drawing attention. If she raced, the Alphas' sharp vision would track her like fleeing prey, and things would only get worse from there. She slipped behind the nearest hut, her body glued to the salvaged metal panels that came from God-knew-where, who-knew-how-long ago. Her heart was making a strong attempt to thump itself right out of her chest, and the tremors that had started in her hands spread up her arms and down her legs.

They were going to catch her. An unmated Omega and a Pack of Alphas. *Oh fuck. Oh fuck. Oh fuck.* A cold sweat beaded along her hairline.

Where had they come from? What were they doing here?

And more importantly, what was she going to do?

By sheer determination, she forced her body to move and get back to her hut. Maybe she could hide there. Between the bonfire and the sharp stench of grain alcohol, maybe their senses would be dulled and they would lose her Omega scent on the wind. Maybe they'd bed a few of the single women in the village and disregard her.

They'd never do that.

No Alpha would fuck a Beta if there was Omega pussy around. She knew that for an absolute fact.

In the hut, she slammed herself against the closed door, her mind spinning in a thousand directions. She had to leave, but where to go? It was night. There were coyotes and wolves and goddamn bears in the woods. And there were wolves right outside her door. She had no food, no lantern, not even a sleeping roll she could take.

She lunged away from the door, scrabbling for her knife with white knuckles. Panicked tears spilled down her cheeks as she crumpled to the floor next to her bed. Five years of running. For nothing. All for nothing.

Kess was trapped.

CHAPTER 4

Hunter

Hunter liked this pup. Heck would be a good addition to their Pack. Strong, growing, and keen, he was ready to leave his parents, whether he knew it yet or not. Hunt saw the signs. As soon as the boy stepped in front of his own father tonight, it had been the end of this chapter of his life. Deep inside, in a place it would take Heck years to recognize, he had lost respect for his Beta father. He might still love the guy, sure, but he wouldn't be able to see him as anything but a weak Beta any longer. And when that happened, the pup had to go.

If he stayed, only strife and struggle would follow. The pup's parents kept sneaking glances as they spoke and sipped the burning alcohol by the fire. Hunt would talk with them if he had to, explain it had to go this way. The moms were always the worst, sobbing and carrying on. He hated that part, but he'd do it. Maybe for the last time. A last parting kindness for this life.

Maybe he'd get a few of the Alphas to hunt some bigger game to leave with this sad village when they vacated tomorrow. He couldn't stand to hang around here more than necessary.

During a lull in conversation, something tickled deep inside his nose. He narrowed his gaze, scanning the rowdy crowd of Betas and Alphas, each mostly keeping to their own kind, except for a few brave Betas engaged with members of his Pack here and there. Nothing out of the place, but... there it was again—that *scent*.

With a hand on Heck's shoulder, Hunter leapt to his feet, his eyes darting around for the source. Sweetness, like... caramel syrup on ice cream he'd had before TheEnd. Yes, that was it. Caramel... and cinnamon. His mouth watered as his nose sought more in the air. But what could it be?

His feet carried him across the clearing to the other side of the fire, tracking. Whatever it was, he had to find it. He had to taste it. He had to know it.

A family of Betas cowered below, petrified faces gaping as he stopped in front of them. The Beta woman clutched a child to her chest as he squatted down, gulping deep breaths into his lungs. The scent was purer here, but what was it? Coming from these Betas?

He gave them a deep sniff and honed in on the little girl. *The hat.* With a swipe, he pulled it from her head, and she began to cry, a pitiful, whining sound. But he couldn't care as he buried his nose in the knit and sucked in the deepest inhale of his entire life.

The scent coated his nose, saturated his senses, and hardened his cock all in an instant.

"Whose hat is this?" he demanded, waving it in front of her face. "Where did you get it?"

The girl cried harder, and an irrational rage beat a rapid pulse behind his eyes. On one hand, he could see himself terrorizing a child like a fucking deranged monster and understood that was a wrong thing to do. But on the other, he was ready to wring it out of her stupid Beta neck. In a life of one hundred and thirty-odd years, he'd rarely been so unhinged.

"It's the teacher's," her mother explained, her voice wobbling. "Kess. Her name is Kess."

"Where is she?" he growled.

The mom pointed across the fire, past some of the pathetic hovels and into the darkness. His Alpha eyesight picked up the outline of a darkened hut hidden behind the others. No fire shone from inside, but something in his chest confirmed that was where he needed to go.

Pulling a half-lit branch from the fire for a makeshift torch, he paced beyond the clearing, aware of the eyes of his Pack brothers on his back. If they knew what was good for them, they'd stay the fuck out of his way right about now. Gripping the hat, he inhaled the scent again, then sought traces of it in the air. It grew stronger as he approached the darkened hut. He knew in his bones what he wanted was nearby.

He couldn't remember ever having wanted something like he wanted what was behind that joke of a door. *Thud, thud, thud.* The entire shelter rocked under the force of his fist, and he heard a stifled gasp from inside, bringing to mind a children's story about a wolf and some pigs and blowing a house down.

Well. He was a fucking wolf. And whatever hid inside was most definitely his prey.

Thud, thud, thud. He pounded harder. "Open up."

Thud, thud, thud. The door rattled off whatever shit it considered hinges and fell apart under his palm. One quick yank, and he tossed it in the grass behind him. The delicious scent surrounded him as he ducked inside, like he'd dove into a caramel river. He wanted to lick it up, every last drop.

Soft crying slowed his movement, and he lifted the torch higher. A woman hunched on the floor, her face buried in her knees and arms wrapped tight around her legs. Black curls rested on her quaking shoulders, so soft and delicate he wanted to rub them all over his face.

Mad, crazy, insane urges.

On the floor was a meager firepit, recently dirt-smothered, but still warm. Forcing calm, he grabbed a log from the corner and tossed it and his torch to build the fire back up. Light flicked up the walls as he stood, slouching in the too-small structure. If he straightened to his full height, he'd bust the roof right off this piece-of-shit hovel.

Fire going, he crouched in front of the woman and attempted to rein in the urgency rolling through him. "Who are you?"

"I'm no one," a small, tinny voice replied. "Please go away."

The answer pissed him off.

He leaned in closer, bordering on looming. "I will not go away. And you will look at me right fucking now."

The voice that came out of his chest did not sound like his. It was deeper, richer, and more growl than actual words. But the woman understood. He knew she did, and he *felt* her cede to the demand. He *felt* her resistance melt through some communication channel he'd never known existed.

Her head rose slowly—forehead, then big, dark eyes swimming with tears, then tear-stained cheeks, then luscious, full lips and a delicate chin. Something slammed into his chest in the same place where the voice had come from, and he suddenly hated the sight of her huddled in the dirt. It was wrong in some indescribable way.

"Get up," he said, circling her arm with his hand and hefting her to her feet. Standing, her head barely reached his chest, and her whole body shook. Small. Small and fine-boned. He tipped forward, bending down and down, even farther down to sample her scent. Dragging his nose down her damp cheek, under the curve of her jaw and along her neck, he breathed in the sweet, intoxicating aroma.

It was the source. She was the source. His body reacted, heat suffusing his skin and tightening his groin. He sucked in another inhale, noting a subtle shift in the smell. Still sweet and alluring, but also salty and biting, tinged with fear. He didn't like it like this. He wanted the sweetness, the pure sweetness, back. His sluggish, scent-crazed brain blinked on, accepting the dispatch from his emphatic dick, the conclusion so obvious as to be ridiculous.

"*Omega.*" He stared deep into her eyes. She met his gaze, which he liked. Afraid, but not cowed. Good. She would be a strong Omega.

A strong Omega just for him.

Blood rushed into his already straining cock. He palmed himself through his clothes for some paltry relief.

31

In a second, he would have to take it out, lest it pound through his pants like the beast it was.

The Omega's eyes followed his hand as he rubbed himself, and her face slackened from forehead to chin. Her mouth fell open. With his other hand, he swiped a path over her lower lip's plush contour. Her eyes hooded and fluttered, and the scent became even more potent with a tangy note over the sweetness.

Slick, his brain shouted at him, and he knew the truth of it. He'd smelled Omega pussy before. He'd sampled it in the rare whorehouses sometimes found on the outskirts of city ruins—whorehouses run by disgusting, corrupt Alphas he'd sooner kill than barter with. And yet, sick with shame and lust, he'd bartered with them for a taste of something only a hint as good as this. Fuck those Alpha bastards to fucking hell. Exploiting Omegas and telling hapless Alphas this was the best Omega cunt they could hope for. No, fuck that. That was a fucking joke.

This. This was the Omega his body had craved for a hundred years.

He slipped his thumb into her mouth and rested it on the moist heat of her tongue. He rubbed there, her lips parting wider and her precious pink tongue presenting itself. He wanted a lot more pink flesh before the night was over.

Grabbing a handful of her shirt, he ripped it to the side, exposing her neck, shoulder, and upper arm. She flinched, but didn't resist as he blinked his eyes to make sense of what he was seeing. There, in the flickering light from the pathetic fire, four or more bite marks marred her beautiful brown skin. Aggression primed his muscles.

He'd been checking for a claiming bite. *A* claiming bite. One, as was customary for a mated pair. Not a mess like this. Horrified, he wrenched down her other sleeve, finding a similar disfigurement, his blood boiling.

Mind grasping for explanations, each one made him sicker than the last. Had one Alpha done this to her? Or a succession of mates? Had she been claimed by an entire *Pack*? He'd heard of barbaric Packs, but nothing like this. Nausea knifed through his guts.

"Where is he?" Hunter demanded, his voice low and lethal.

She said nothing, her dark eyes ringed with white.

"Where," he began again, his thumb stroking over the heinous marks, "is the Alpha who did this? I'll fight him, and I will kill him."

"He's dead," she whispered.

In a flash, Hunt collared her neck and pushed her against the flimsy wall. It bowed and flexed with the impact, but held better than the door. A small yelp left her lips, and he enjoyed a sick thrill at her limp submission. He held her with only a small amount of pressure, just enough to make his presence known, not enough to actually hinder her airway.

He wasn't a total psycho.

"Don't lie for that weak fucking bastard," Hunt seethed.

He glanced up at her face, all the arousal that had been there erased and replaced by a quaking shame. Hunt's nostrils flared, seeking any scent of dishonesty. He found none. She canted her head away from him, not meeting his eyes, slumping under his hold. Her defeat softened his inner turmoil.

She was telling the truth. Lanced with tenderness, he righted her clothes, covering the marks from view.

"An Alpha did this to you? These marks? Or were there,"—the words choked him—"more?"

He released her, and her head fell back to rest on the wall, exposing her beautiful neck. Soft and delicate, he ached to lave a path along the smooth, perfect column. His raging erection signaled its support of this plan. As if he had any doubt.

"Just him," she said, daring to meet his eyes with a touch of defiance. "Are you going to add yours now? I should tell you, I'm barren." Her voice strengthened with every word. "I will bear you no pups. My Alpha—"

"The *dead* Alpha," Hunt corrected, not wanting to hear any "my Alphas" coming out of her mouth to mean anyone but him.

"Brock," she conceded, "kept trying to 'fix' our bond. He thought I wasn't doing it right. So he…" Her shoulder lifted in resignation and indication of what he did.

The fucking dirt-eating, scum-sucking bastard. That motherfucker had this Omega in his bed and chose to gnaw her body like a piece of fucking *rawhide*? Because she couldn't give him pups? He should be glad he was dead, or Hunt would track him down and pull his intestines out his motherfucking nose.

"I'm a defective Omega and have nothing to offer you. Please…" She took a shuddering breath. "Please let me stay here. I'm old and barren. I'm no use to you."

Dark intent swirled his body. It guided him one step closer, crowding her against the wall. He angled his pelvis into hers and ground against her stomach. Angling forward, he circled her neck again, tilting her head to the side so he could lick her fragrant neck. Her salty-sweet taste exploded on his tongue, and he groaned into her flesh before whispering in her ear, "I think we both know that's not true."

CHAPTER 5

Kess

Anguish infused her body and clouded her vision. Sensation upon conflicting sensation assaulted her. Hot, cold, tight, loose, jittery, languid, free, bound. Her Omega nature violently rousing out of dormancy complicated every thought in her head.

The Alpha's massive body pinned hers, grinding his impossibly hard cock into her belly. As if she needed the reminder. As if she hadn't been aware of it from the moment he'd burst through her feeble dwelling, smelling of potency and demand. Her hat clutched in his fist, he'd tracked her scent. There must be some irony there, for her favorite hat to cause her destruction.

His heavy paw cuffed her neck—gently, if it could be called that, but enough to command. Like a kitten hoisted by its scruff, her body slackened at the contact and, worst of all, slick leaked from between her legs. Even she could smell it now, its sweetness rising above the sharp Alpha scent that saturated the air, woodsy and green and seasoned with the ripe tang of sexual hunger. Her Omega drank him in, his aroma delicious and electrifying. Even forcing the appeal from her mouth had been a struggle, her vocal cords and lips and breath rebelling against the plea for clemency from his attentions.

That was the fucking hell of the whole thing. As much as she wanted to resist, she would never be able to. Her Omega nature wanted his attentions. Craved his attentions. Insisted it would die without them.

Kess allowed herself to meet his gaze—the same Alpha she had spotted talking to Heck—and marveled at his raw, uncut beauty. Lowered brows, snarling mouth, and piercing eyes fixed on her face. His skin was lighter than hers, which made him stand out in the AfterEnd, where most people were shades of black and brown. Sun lines feathered from his eyes, adding fierceness to his already austere demeanor. But most notable of all was his hair. Backlit by the fire he'd built up, silvery gray laced through it. Starting from his temples, where the gray had overtaken the brown, it streaked back over his entire head, gilding him like a crown.

All Alphas were handsome in their brutal, rough-hewn way. But this one stole the breath from her lungs.

"Are you the one they call Kess, Omega?" His voice softened from a growl to an almost-purr. Her sex buzzed, recognizing her name on his lips and reveling in it.

"Yes, Alpha."

His eyes searched her face. "You were hiding from me."

"No." Her lips raced to defend against his accusation, instinctively deflecting Alpha displeasure. "Not from you, in particular…" she added weakly.

His head dipped out of her vision, and his voice rumbled in her ear, "You can't hide from me, Omega."

He sniffed along her face and licked behind her ear, sending shockwaves of desire in all directions. Oh God, he felt so *good*. The tips of her breasts tightened into mean, aching points, abraded by the rough texture of her shirt. They screamed for his suckling, the one thing that would soothe them.

Oblivious, his lips danced along her throat, down to her clavicle and over her shoulder, sucking and nipping at the delicate skin. A hot, soft tongue glided over her scars, mouthing them as he went, as if to lick them clean and erase the blemishes. Or maybe he was scent-marking her, depositing himself, painting over and negating the other Alpha. Soothing her past hurts with the tender attention. The poignancy plowed through her, and a single tear dripped from one eye and rolled down her cheek.

His head jerked up as if he had scented the salty drop. Warmth shined from his gaze as he licked the drop away, the damp replaced by the wet touch of his tongue.

A pitiful whimper snuck past her lips, her Omega fully entranced. "Who are you, Alpha?"

Instinct, survival or otherwise, propelled her to ask the question, to move the connection forward. Her Omega wanted to belong to this Alpha. Her Omega body would've responded to any Alpha who'd knocked down the door and growled in her ear, as she'd submitted to Brock when he'd cornered her as a young, burgeoning Omega and stolen her from her family.

That's what she hated most.

Her Omega nature robbed her of any semblance of choice. Beta women could flirt and court and fall in love;

Omegas could only succumb to their nature. Like with Brock, this Alpha summoned, and her Omega responded. The fact that she was Kess, a whole person with thoughts and feelings and hopes and dreams, was beside the point.

Freeing her neck, his enormous hands grasped her upper arms, fastening her body to his. Body heat blasted through her threadbare clothing and seared the front of her chest. The tight points of her nipples complained even more. She would die right then for a chance to rub them against his bare chest.

Then again, it hadn't been exactly like this with Brock. That had felt confusing and exhilarating, like being swept up in a wave of dangerous, awakening desire. This… this Alpha was the ocean itself. Powerful, infinite, relentless. His body, his scent, his presence scrambled her brain. Yet she wanted to dive in and drown all the same.

"Hunter." The grumbled name vibrated from his chest to hers, and more moisture poured into her already-damp pants. She'd forgotten how juicy her sex got in an Alpha's presence.

Hunter. The name fit. He'd tracked and hunted her, and now she was thoroughly snared in his trap. At least, her Omega was caught. She, Kess, the small portion of herself clinging to independence, clung to freedom.

His lips tensed, and he moved his eyes around her shack. She felt his mood darken as he examined every corner and inch of humble space.

"What are you doing in this shithole village?" he asked when his gaze landed on the bumpy rag-stuffed pallet she used as a bed. "You're Omega. Your place is with a Pack."

Flashes of her life in a Pack elbowed through her arousal haze. The isolation and loneliness. The pain with each monthly disappointment. Brock's increasing frustration, the evidence of which she bore on her skin. She ground her back teeth with indignation, affronted by this oh-so-typical Alpha audacity. After seeing her scars, how could he ask a stupid question like that? Or did he just not care? Was that brief show of compassion just that—a show?

"This shithole is better than any fucking *Pack*," she spat.

Sharp eyes snapped back to hers, and she gulped around the ball of fear in her throat. The moment strained under his tight regard and the ire she'd provoked diminishing a hair, replaced by a flicker of approval.

"You have a mouth on you, Omega." His lip quirked up at the corner. "I could think of a thing or two I could do with a smart mouth like yours."

Oh God, yes, do them, her Omega begged as more wetness rolled down her thigh. Kess braced against it and grasped at the small voice inside telling her to resist, to not give in, to not let five years of running and hiding go without a fight. That small voice said maybe he would give up if she didn't immediately yield. Maybe he'd see her defect and lose interest.

That voice opened its mouth and snapped, "It's not like I can stop you, *Alpha*."

At this, his quirked lip deepened into a lopsided dimple, his eyes sparking with amusement. "No, you can't." He stepped back from her, as much as he could in the small space, and flung a hand around the room. "Get your shit, we're leaving."

Kess' small voice wailed and her Omega sang, sending wave after wave of conflicting emotions through her body.

That was it, then. There would be no escape. He was taking her wherever he wanted, whenever he wanted, their destination a mystery she couldn't muster interest in. Wherever they were going, her thoughts or opinions made no difference.

"Now," he barked when she didn't hop-to fast enough.

She winced at the implied violence in his tone. She'd never known an Alpha to strike an Omega outright, but she had witnessed Omegas forcefully handled and even disciplined at the whims of a displeased Alpha. They were brutes by definition. No use getting starry-eyed about this one because he'd managed to hold off fucking her within the first ten minutes of their acquaintance. That put him a league above Brock, but that wasn't saying much. As much as Hunter exerted firm control over his rather assertive arousal, his tendencies and proclivities remained a cipher.

Stepping past him, she lifted her comb and the brush she used to clean her teeth. "Things for the night, or will I be coming back—"

"Get. Your. Shit." He folded his arms over his chest and leveled an expectant glare.

Kess grabbed a knapsack and started shoving her sole possessions inside—rudimentary toiletries, the silky scarf she used to wrap her hair, her one change of clothes. She stooped and plucked her rainbow hat off the floor where he'd dropped it. The hat had ruined her life, but it was still a good hat.

"You made those?"

She followed his eyes to the stack of woven baskets. "Yes."

He responded with a grunt, and she resumed gathering items. The few books she owned sat next to her bed. She snuck a sidelong glance at him, gauging his rapidly shifting mood and if she could brave another question. Brock had been illiterate and rejected her offers to teach him. Who knew if this Alpha had any learning, or if he was brute stacked on brute?

Somehow, she suspected he wasn't, but she chastised herself for wishful thinking. Deciding against asking permission, she grabbed the books and crammed them into the bulging knapsack, working them down to the bottom beneath her clothes. Hopefully he wouldn't notice. Worst case scenario, he threw them in the fire. She'd survived that once before, and she'd survive it again if it came to that.

"Gimme your bag."

Kess cinched the top closed and tied it off. Hefting it from the floor, she suppressed a grimace at its weight as she handed it over. But Hunter swung it over his shoulder as if it weighed nothing. The pack landed on his broad back, a small thing on the muscled expanse, like a wart on a frog.

"Oh!" She remembered, spinning around and pulling the lid off her buried food storage hole. The cloth Heck had given her waited there, where she'd repacked and left it earlier. She grabbed the small packet and held it up to show the Alpha. "Some food. Not much."

His nostrils flared, and another glower descended. "Leave it."

Jak's dismissive comment, *No one would throw away food, stupid*, rang through her head. Despite chastising him, she abided the sentiment. Even small amounts of food were precious in the AfterEnd. Maybe not to this Alpha, though. Maybe his Pack had food aplenty and this paltry offering hardly mattered. That would fit, wouldn't it? Alphas taking whatever they wanted, hoarding resources while others starved.

She shrugged. "It's just an egg and a little dried meat."

"I said leave it, Omega. You only take food from me now, you got it?"

"Oh." She held onto the bundle. After years of near-starvation, her fingers refused to relinquish the scant sustenance.

With a muttered curse, he snatched the cloth and tossed it back in the hole, then seized her arm in one smooth movement.

"Can you go nicely, or should I make it easy on myself and pick you up?"

Kess said a wordless goodbye to the home that had been her sad sanctuary. Nothing special, but it had been hers alone.

At times, she'd imagined moving on from the village, maybe to a larger, less religious Beta settlement where she might feel safe enough to make some actual friends. Now that would never happen. Instead, the village would witness her being marched away by an intimidating Alpha into a future of who-knows-what. A few would deduce her Omega nature, revealing her lie for all to see. She didn't care about that so much; she'd done what she needed to do to survive. But her students… she hated leaving them like this, with no explanation or chance to share what they meant to her. Or even to say goodbye.

Forcing back the threatening tears, she bent her head forward in resignation. "I can walk."

CHAPTER 6

Hunter

The Omega had been living in squalor. *His* Omega had been living in squalor. Because, whether she liked it or not—whether *he* liked it or not—she was his, and there would be no separating from here on out.

How quickly things had changed. One whiff of that cinnamon-caramel aroma and all of his molecules had oriented toward the source. A rare pang of anxiety poked him in the chest at the happenstance of the whole thing, and her hidden-in-plain-sight ruse irked him. What was that Beta child even doing with her ridiculous hat? Without it, would the Omega have been able to hide from his Alpha senses enough to pass unnoticed? What if another one of his Pack had found her first?

The last one was easy, at least. He would've fought and killed them for her. No question. He'd been around Omegas in the past. He'd personally sniffed them out, but no Omega scent had ever grabbed him by the balls and hauled him across a village like a madman before.

Why had it taken the hat to attract his attention? An Alpha could scent an Omega within a half-mile, per his rudimentary estimates over the years. She'd been just beyond the clearing the entire time he'd spoken with that pup, and… nothing. Not until the damned hat came into an unavoidable range.

Barren, she'd said. Defective. He didn't give one single fuck about babies—who could bring a child into this world?—but was her barrenness related to the subtlety of her scent? He wished he knew.

Holding her arm, he guided her to the Alpha campsite, instinctively steering her around roots and holes in the pitch-black night. Her Omega senses would be better than Betas', but still not as sharp as his. They neared the encampment, and he was relieved to see his Pack had made a fire and set up their tents. He'd made that a condition of this adventure—waterproof accommodations for the entire Pack. He could sleep rough, but—fuck it—he didn't want to.

Colt knew the drill and ensured the Pack cared for the horses and established the camp before heading back to the shithole village. Nothing worse than trying to organize a bunch of drunken idiot Alphas. Although that village did not have nearly the quantity of spirits needed to get his Pack even slightly buzzed. At best, they'd warm their bellies and maybe sleep a little deeper. Good. Fewer awake to listen to him and his Omega.

The Omega stiffened at the sight of the other Alphas lounging around their fire. He shushed her with a soothing purr emanating from his chest, gratified as her muscles relaxed under his grip. She had nothing to fear from his Pack, but maybe her last one had made her believe otherwise. Anger burned the back of his throat. He'd get her to tell him where to find this other Pack, and maybe he'd take his and go mete out some justice for his Omega, dead Alpha or not.

Fuck, what was happening to him? He sounded like fucking Sloan—rash, cocksure, and hungry for a fight. While he'd never shied away from bloodying his knuckles—you didn't get to the top of the Pack otherwise—Hunt prided himself on being more intelligent and civilized than other Alphas. He'd lived before TheEnd and knew what actual civilization looked like. Fuck, he'd gone to *college*. Sometimes he wondered if he was the last man on Earth who ever had.

"Ho! Alpha of Alphas." Grinning, Mick lifted a palm in greeting. "Who you got there?"

Cursing at the diversion from his plan to get the Omega back to his tent pronto, Hunter wove a path to the fire, where Mick sat with Dev and Van. Downwind and ten yards away, their noses twitched and their eyes trained on the Omega. Interesting. They'd scented her better than he had an hour ago. It wasn't just his him, then; her scent was getting stronger.

Van blew a low whistle. "An Omega all the way out here?"

Hunter growled and snapped a ferocious bite, making his intentions crystal-fucking-clear. They all slouched under the modest display of dominance. Satisfying.

He'd need to assert his primacy more than once over the coming days. As usual, an unmated Omega was a fucking pain. And if she went into Heat, then he'd have a real mess on his hands. Only one way to handle it—quickly make her a mated Omega.

"You find any more?" Mick asked, frank avarice in his eyes.

"Hey, gorgeous," Van addressed the Omega with a shit-eating grin, "you got any friends?"

The shit-eating grin lasted for the approximate two seconds it took Hunt to drop the Omega's pack, haul Van to his feet, and slam a fist into his face, followed by one to his guts—and, grabbing the back of his neck, a knee to his nose. The Omega squeaked behind him, and he glanced at her startled face while Van slumped away. Whining with submission but still upright, he'd have a black eye tomorrow and wear it with pride. Hunt's Pack was tough.

Hunt glared at the two Alphas at the fire and a few others who'd popped their heads out of various tents. "Any other stupid fucking questions?" he bellowed, making murderous eye contact with each of them. He paced a few feet closer, spreading his arms wide. "Any of you mongrels want to come be cute with my Omega? Come on out and let's get this over with so you can lick your wounds and listen to me fuck her."

The Omega's breath hitched, and a fresh burst of her scent touched his nose, her arousal heightened after his display of dominance. Defective his hairy white ass. Her responses were fucking perfect.

A solid minute lapsed, during which he stared every last Alpha down, their necks craning and postures deflating one by one. Good. They'd tell their Packmates and keep the camp quiet. He didn't want any more bullshit tonight.

Snatching the Omega's pack, he extended his hand to her and grunted approval when she slid her palm into his. The dominance demonstration had not only been for his

Alpha brothers. She might as well know he ranked Alpha of Alphas in this Pack.

And that fucking was on the evening's agenda.

As usual, his tent had been placed at the periphery of the camp. Not for privacy—there was no pretense or need of privacy here—but for security. The elder Alphas occupied the perimeter as their senses were most honed. If anything came tromping through the woods, he would hear it first, asleep or not. Although tonight, the others would need to be on alert as his senses were fully saturated with ripe Omega.

Hunt untied the tent flaps and tossed her knapsack inside before bending to remove her shoes. Her tattered boots were held together by more straps and ties than actual boot material. Another thing he'd need to remedy.

Standing, he held the flap open for her. Light from the fire tickled the entrance, but blackness inside lurked like a cave. The Omega hesitated at the threshold, as if afraid this became the point of no return for her. As if once she passed through on her own volition, she ceded everything to him. Little did she know that point had been crossed when he'd ripped the door off her pathetic excuse for a hut.

"Go on, Kess," he said softly, adding a hint of purr to her name along with a palm to her back. He brought his lips to her ear and was rewarded with a feminine shiver. "I won't bite… not yet, anyway."

CHAPTER 7

Kess

Kess's body was one giant, exposed nerve ending. Ducking into the shelter, her skin burned, her heart raced, and her sex tingled. Watching Hunter unleash shouldn't have stirred her as much as it did. And yet... The cool efficiency of his discipline recalled an animal she'd read about once in a book about reptiles. Pit Viper, it was called, an animal that waited in the shadows, all coiled menace and barely leashed lethality, to ambush its prey.

As she rubbed her arms, Kess' eyes adjusted to the darkness. She sat on a surprisingly plush bedroll in the primitive but dry space. His rich, woodsy scent lingered in the bedclothes, and she resisted an urge to press her nose into them for a bigger, purer hit. This was his tent, then. In her prior Pack, unmated Alphas often bunked together, while the ones with Omegas were afforded separate spaces. As Alpha of Alphas of this Pack, which she now understood him to be, it made sense he'd claim a sizeable lodging for his own. The tent afforded enough room for him to sit up and comfortably move around, but not much more, and with the two of them in it, she'd no doubt sleep pressed up against him. That's if she would be sleeping at all.

She doubted it.

Excited quakes tingled low in her belly—her body's instinctive reaction to Hunter, his scent, his proprietary display of aggression with his Pack brother. Feelings she hadn't experienced in years, certainly not since her escape, and maybe not even before. The less she wanted him, the stronger his effect on her.

Rustling noises came from outside the tent. Then the flaps parted and he was there, her muscles tightening and responding to his presence. His smell and the warmth radiating off him revealed he'd removed his shirt. Kess swallowed back a mouthwatering urge to lick his bare skin from stomach to chin. She fought the yearning, reminding herself she didn't need to know the taste of his skin or its texture against her lips. Her Omega nature craved that information, but she, Kess, didn't care. He'd have his way with her, that was inevitable, but she could hold back, stay aloof, and preserve something of herself. In fact, she had to.

The Alpha—*Hunter*—prowled to the back of the tent, snagging her around the waist and depositing her between his legs, her back to his front. Her back stiffened at the contact, resisting the allure of his heat and the strength that seduced her without a single word uttered. If he noted her tense response, it didn't slow him down. Tree-trunk thighs caged her in, and he yanked and pulled to divest her of her jacket. He balled it up with a brief, disgusted snort and threw it outside. *Okay, then…*

Her shirt came next, baring her greedy skin to the full force of his. Crisp chest hair rasped over her shoulder blades, tempting her to lean back and fully melt into him.

It was such a small thing to press her body to his and soak up everything on offer. To satisfy the Omega need coursing through her body, completely unconcerned and unbothered by her resistance. Resistance that was fast becoming futile. She squeezed her eyes shut against the erotic onslaught.

Undeterred, Hunter ripped through the tattered bindings she used for breast support with an even more displeased rumble. That was short-lived, though, his displeasure replaced by a noise of deep, rolling satisfaction when his palms captured her breasts. She gasped, eyes snapping open, her Omega fully awake and on board with his ministrations. Kess shivered and quaked under the strain, sighing in tortured relief as she finally gave up and wilted into the broad expanse of his chest. Her small resistance crushed by the incoming tsunami of pure want.

A soft, closed-lipped moan broke from her throat, and the Alpha responded with an approving, domineering growl. It vibrated from his chest into hers and buzzed down his arms, into the fingers that plumped and pinched her sensitive nipples.

"Good, Omega." He nosed his way through her curls to croon in her ear while his palms hefted her breasts. "We'll get these fattened up in no time." He slid his massive hands down her body and over her waist and to take big handfuls of her inner thighs and wrench them apart. "These too. No more starvation for you, Omega. Not now, not ever."

She squirmed under his touch, arching her back into the hard bar behind her, barely able to register the promises he was making. Starvation? Fattening? Food was a distant concern, something for another time, when thick male fingers weren't fiddling with her waistband and slipping a hand inside to cup her. A plaintive gasp shot out of her and no doubt echoed through the camp, but she couldn't find it anywhere within herself to care. This Alpha had turned her upside-down and sideways, transformed her into a creature composed solely of base, depraved need.

He chuckled darkly in her ear, his fingertips lightly grazing the hot, desperate flesh. "Are you hungry? Do you want to eat now, Omega?"

Her hips bucked and strained, seeking pressure and relief in his inexorable grip. She complained with an indignant whine. And, just as fast, his palm withdrew from the tight confines of her pants and spanked her pussy in one, two, three, sharp slaps. Atop her soaked clothes, the soggy smacks cracked in the air, which only made it more humiliating and electrifying and nearly sent her into a climax.

"Asked you a question, Omega," he said, his voice dripping with amusement as a single finger sketched a weak, teasing path up her seam, as if mocking her for hanging so near the precipice.

"No, not hungry," she breathed, hooking her waistband to shove her pants down and kick them off.

He let her do it, more indulgent chuckles rumbling from his chest. Once she'd freed her legs, she reclined back into his body, fully naked and open, and so, so turned on.

Hunter's hands mapped her exposed body everywhere he could reach, thighs to hips to waist to breasts to shoulders to arms to hands. Lacing their fingers together, he brought them up to her breasts, encouraging her to present the globes while he massaged and pinched with more concentrated intent. Intent to drive her straight into madness.

"I can't wait to see all this in the daylight," he mused. "The sun shining down, toasting your skin and baking your delicious scent like fresh cookies. I'd wait, except..." He snickered at his own joke. "I don't want to."

"Please," she whispered.

"Little Omega has changed her mind." He pinched her pointed tips hard, making her cry out with the pleasure-pain of it. "Not hiding now, is she? Didn't take too long, did it? Till she was begging for some Alpha cock. *My* Alpha cock. Isn't that right, Kess?"

He breathed her name on a laugh, an open mockery of her quashed rebellion. As if to force her to admit that Kess and her Omega were one in the same, whether she liked it or not.

"Yes," she moaned, her pelvis pulsing in the air, into nothing but fruitless frustration.

In one swift movement, he grasped her waist and raised her off the ground as he slid flat on his back and settled her pussy over his face. She yelped, first in surprise, then again in relief as his intent became clear.

"Oh God," she breathed, her hands braced on his wide, solid abdomen and her thighs quaking to hold herself still and not just grind her way to satisfaction. It wouldn't take much, but somehow, she knew he wouldn't want her to *take* her pleasure. He'd want to bestow it like a magnanimous king.

Which, thankfully, was his plan. With a visceral growl, he hauled her hips down and dove in, licking and tasting and lapping at the over-sensitized tissues. Not toying or teasing, he *devoured* and lit her entire body on fire. Massive hands securing her in place and thumbs parting and lightly stroking her inner lips, his tongue dove deeper and deeper, drinking up the slick that poured from her core. The contrast between his greedy, open-mouthed feasting and the delicate, almost reverent thumb caress undid her.

Relaxing, she tested the feel of a small, tight grind. This earned her an enthusiastic growl which reverberated from his lips up through her womb and buzzed her aching nipples. Again her hips pulsed into him, seeking more sensation and a remedy for the steadily-building torture. Sharp prickles from his whiskers bit into her delicate bud and she didn't care, every sensation welcome as she surfed the exquisite edge before release.

Lost to everything but the swipe of his tongue over her sex, her arms collapsed. Breasts flattened on his solid abdomen, her face brushed against his enormous dick. Even through pants, the heat and command of it warmed her cheek, and one lungful of his concentrated, musky Alpha scent cascaded her over the precipice into a shuddering climax. Nose snuggled into his cock, she sucked great gulps of that intoxicating aroma as her shuddering release drove on and on and further and further.

Her thighs quivered and shook, and sounds wrenched from her throat she'd never heard before. They may have been groans, they may have been screams; she wasn't sure and didn't much care. She'd moved to some other place, to a place beyond struggle and shame. Fully surrendered, her Omega sang with happiness and, if there was a separate part of her, it had been obliterated by her shattering climax.

She'd been re-arranged in some fundamental way, the old picture shuffled and the lines redrawn to create something new.

Hunter's hands locked her in place through her tremors, denying her body's request to jerk away from the stimulation. He refocused his efforts away from her sensitive nub but continued his relentless consuming.

Still shaking from her epic release, she whined, "No… I can't again…"

"You can." He slapped her hip, making her jump. "You will. Get my cock out, Omega."

Levering herself up on limp arms, she worked open the fastenings and caught his monster dick, hot and heavy, in her hand. Compelled to explore, she brushed him first with her cheek and then her nose, rubbing him all over her face until, unable to hold back, she licked at the fluid beading on the slit, eliciting a deep grunt in the midst of his ongoing feasting. His taste coated her tongue, a salted concentration of his deep, rich scent. She went back for more, gliding his hard length over her tongue.

She loved it. *Oh, God*, she loved it. And she hated that she loved it, but that was a thought for another time, another day. In the darkness of the tent, her other senses heightened and honed. His scent richer, his taste stronger, his skin hotter. Her body spasmed and trembled, and her lips groped for more, more, *more*. The silky, hard feel of him in her mouth was the only thing keeping her from spinning out and dissolving into the heavenly sky.

She sucked him harder, and Hunter grunted, distracting her as he redoubled his efforts and again spiraled her arousal higher and higher. Another peak approached, brought into focus by his skilled efforts, his Alpha scent and his lip-stretching cock. A hungry *hmmm* was the only noise she could make as he slipped two fingers into her body and pumped them slowly while his tongue flicked against her clit. Mindless with pleasure, she tried to attend to him but failed, only able to hum her approval and suckle him weakly through another frantic orgasm, her cries muted and muffled around his dick.

"That's enough for now, Omega," Hunter said, giving her a few parting laps as he guided her off his face and away from his cock. Disoriented and dizzy, Kess rolled off him while he divested himself of his pants and knelt in front of her. "Lie on your back," he commanded and guided her head between his knees, their prior positions swapped.

His heavy cock bobbed in front of her face, liquid dribbling off the tip and trailing down to paint her lips. She licked the heady taste into her mouth.

With a dark huff, he fisted himself and dragged the tip over her lips. "You want it, don't you? Can you take what I give you, Omega?"

She whimpered an assent, her mouth open and waiting for him to stuff it full. Thick male fingertips stroked her cheeks almost tenderly. "Yeah, I think you can," he said, his voice thickened with lust. "You're a good Omega. You weren't hiding, were you? You were waiting. Waiting for me."

With that, he pushed in and stretched her lips beyond what she'd managed before. Even with saliva pooled and ready, he only slid a spare halfway in. But he pumped in and out, fisting the base of his cock and squeezing the girth that would become his knot when he decided to fuck her properly. Like all Alphas, the root of his cock would swell when he climaxed inside an Omega, locking behind the pelvic bone and sealing them together until the knot subsided.

She'd never given Brock's knot much thought; it simply was. But watching Hunter work himself in sure strokes, the idea of his hot, bulging knot wedged inside of her made her crazy. Kess swallowed, tried to gulp more down, as greedy for him as he was to give it to her. He shifted on his knees, angling to gain another inch while his hands cradled her cheeks, moving her mouth where he wanted.

This pleased him, and he cursed in the cramped space, now warm and humid with their exertions. His hips worked above her, his thighs like slabs of meat as she licked and sucked and drooled and rejoiced in every pump. Wet and straining, his cock slid over her tongue and into her throat, stretching and gagging. He moaned and grunted and groaned as it swelled even further in her mouth.

His movements turned jerky, stuttering, and his groans even louder. Surely everyone in the camp—maybe even in the village—would hear her Alpha fucking her face. *Good*, she thought, defiant. *Let them.*

Hunter grabbed at her breasts. And grabbed was the word, not a polite tease meant to arouse—no, it was a hungry, sloppy grope that belied his razor-thin edge. He squeezed them tight, to the border of pain, holding them as he reached a heaving finish and fluid gushed her mouth.

She choked and sputtered as it overflowed onto her cheeks and dripped down her chin. Hunter filled his palms with the overflow and rubbed it on her body. Over her neck and shoulders, painting over her scars with a new Alpha marking. This seemed to prolong his climax further, causing more spurting as he pulled out and shot onto her breasts and abdomen. He massaged that in too, his throbbing sex a heavy monument above her face. An object of beauty. And lust. And worship. His taste lingered on her tongue, and already, she wanted more.

Maybe sensing her desire, Hunter swiped the last sticky stream off her chest and brought it to her lips. She took it eagerly and cleaned his finger of every last drop. Hunter grunted his approval and caressed her cheek with the back of his hand.

"Time to rest, Omega," he said, lying down and pulling her sticky body on top of his.

Disappointment fluttered around the edges of her awareness. That was it? He wasn't going to mate with her? Bite her? Mark his claim? Give her his knot?

He cradled her head to his chest, and she breathed in his intoxicating scent, now enriched with heady sex exertion and the scent of his spend. Maybe there was some reassurance in this small sexual introduction; maybe he envisioned some measured plan to claim her later, under different circumstances. He'd said something about daylight…

From deep in his chest came a comforting, pleasant purr that interrupted this train of thought. Reassured, a happy sigh whispered across her lips. Overcome with exhaustion and contentment, her lids drooped, and she had no further thoughts for many, many hours.

CHAPTER 8

Hunt

The Omega collapsed in his arms. His ripe and redolent scent overlaid hers, and he wallowed in bone-deep satisfaction of the novel combination. In his old life, before TheEnd, he would've been ashamed to handle and defile a woman with such possessive barbarity. But, like many things, that was before. Back when he was Paul Jason Hunter, an affable emergency room doctor who biked to work, loved his grill, and played ultimate frisbee on weekends.

Not the hulking beast he was now. A beast who'd bloody a man's nose, then shamelessly fuck a woman in a nylon tent for every creature in a two-mile radius to hear.

Not a woman. *An Omega.*

To be fair, he'd fucked Omegas before. It became hard not to want it once the Alpha transformation took place, realigning his entire existence around the precious compliment to his brutal nature. He'd succumbed to the base depravities of his Ruts and excised the lust-insane demon they called forth. But the mating bond shit, he'd been skeptical of, quite frankly. Sure, other Alphas in his region had found Omegas to mate and keep long-term. They would wax poetic about some sort of bond, marked by mutual bite marks shared between lovers, but he'd questioned the whole thing as laughable, and judged those

Alphas as jealous and greedy for wanting to lock an Omega down rather than let the Omegas make their own choices. Granted, the AfterEnd wasn't safe for Omegas—or anyone, for that matter—but in particular, the sweet-smelling, biologically-compatible Omegas.

He'd had a similar jaded view of marriage back before TheEnd. He liked to screw around, and why not? Why limit himself to one pussy when variety was the spice of life, right? Although that did lead to the inevitable dry spells, which was why he supposed some men succumbed to monogamy and marriage—to avoid those.

He shook his head at what he used to consider a dry spell. If he'd known then he'd be alive for over a hundred years and go literal decades without any one option other than his own hand, he might have hurled himself into the ocean a lot sooner.

A peaceful snore slipped out of the Omega. In an instant, the thought of suicide churned Hunter's stomach with nausea. He tightened the arm securing her to his chest as if *she* needed reassurance from the suicidal thought. Now that he'd found this Omega—*Kess*, he needed to call her Kess—dying was the absolute last thing he wanted. Mating bond or whatever bullshit notwithstanding, he wasn't about to let her go. At least, not before he claimed her cunt properly, in the full light of day and with more room to move around than this blasted tent.

He'd held back. His tongue lapping and drinking down her sweet, earthy taste by the mouthful, all he could think about was plunging his cock right into that tight, searing hot space. But then he'd slipped a finger in and, despite his lust-crazed insanity, grew concerned about said tightness. Even being an Omega, he'd need to take some care and pace the screwing so as not to hurt her. Who knew how long it had been since she'd been thoroughly fucked? He wanted—no, *needed*—it to be good for her.

Just like he needed to turn this Pack around and return to the semblance of civilization they'd built at Morris Hill. He'd had enough of this churchy, backwoods weirdness. He wanted his Omega in his cabin, all to himself, preferably before she went into a Heat cycle.

When was her last Heat cycle? He ought to ask her. Ought to ask her a lot of things, but they'd have time for all that in the morning. With that, Hunt drifted off to blissful, dreamless sleep.

Dawn shone through the tent material when he next opened his eyes. One of the lighter sleepers in camp due to his sensitive hearing, Hunt usually beat everyone up. Not today, however, as he heard the morning rustlings to build up the fire and start the grub for the Pack. He knew all the sounds his Packmates made as they went about waking up—scratching, muttering, farting, griping about whatever-the-fuck. Today, though, they made a notable effort to keep the noise down, probably on account of Hunt and his Omega. A smile cracked his lips, and he caressed her naked back in a gentle attempt to rouse her.

His dick woke up as well, already hard and complaining, but there wouldn't be time for any more of that today. They needed to roll on out of this hellhole. The sooner, the better.

"Oh-ho, what do we have here?" Sloan's belligerent voice broke the early morning peace. "You lost, little pup? Looking for your mama? You should check my tent; I think I saw her there last."

Oh hell, of course the pup would run into arguably the biggest asshole in the Pack first.

"I'm looking for the Alpha of Alphas," Heck said, his voice clear and unbothered by Sloan's shit-talking.

With a reluctant sigh, Hunt shifted the Omega off his body and woke her the rest of the way up. Round, wide-set eyes as deep brown as rich, fertile soil watched him, and he swore his heart skipped a beat... or ten.

She was fucking gorgeous. Last night he'd thought she'd been pretty enough in the dim firelight, but now, in the watery morning, she took his breath away. Her skin, smooth and flawless and tawny brown, made him want to spend the rest of his life worshiping every last inch of her. Bleary bedroom eyes, a distinctive nose, and lush, pillowed lips—those he'd sampled, at least—completed her beauty.

But he hadn't sampled her lips to his satisfaction. So consumed with the urge to glut himself on her intoxicating slick, he'd forgotten to bestow upon her a single kiss. What an asshole.

And now there wasn't time.

"Time to get up, Omega," he said, his voice gruff with regret and recrimination. "Get dressed and come outside. I gotta take care of some shit."

She waited while he yanked on his pants and fastened them over his raging hardon. The voices outside the tent were escalating, the energy of a fight thrumming in the air. As Alpha of Alphas, they'd wait for him to start the initiation, but he didn't want to delay more than necessary.

"Get moving," he said, cracking Kess on her shapely ass. She jumped with a little squeak, and it took every ounce of his control not to roll her over right then and shove his dick inside. Grumbling to himself, he grabbed the rest of his clothes and boots outside the tent.

Jeers and taunts rose from the Pack, encircled around the newest member, Heck.

"So what's it gonna be, mama's boy?" Sloan was still running his mouth. "Who you feel like having your ass kicked by today?"

"'Mornin', Alpha," Colt muttered as Hunt sidled up, fastening his belt. "Pup showed up."

"Yeah, I heard." Hunt ran his eyes over the young Alpha recruit, standing in the middle of the restless, excited Pack. To his credit, he stood straight, and Hunt could tell he fought to keep his muscles loose and relaxed, trying his best not to react to the loads of shit they were heaping on him as part of the ritual.

"Settle down." Hunt raised his voice, and all eyes turned toward him, Van's sporting a rather fine shiner. "This here is Heck. He's gonna be joining us from here on out. That is, once he fights one of you assholes." Hunt pointed at Heck. "You get to choose who you wanna fight. Any Alpha here will gladly take you on and show us what you got." He grinned ferociously. "Myself included."

The pup's face paled at this, but he visibly steeled himself to make the choice. It was a shit bargain all the way around. If the pup chose to fight Hunt or one of the bigger Alphas, he'd most surely get his ass kicked into next week, and maybe even end up with a broken arm or worse for his trouble. If he chose the youngest pup, Alek, he might win, or at least not get demolished, but he'd lose the respect of the Pack for not going up against a bigger Alpha. What the pup may or may not have realized was that it didn't matter if he won the fight, only that he demonstrated he could take a beating like an Alpha and not some Beta bitch.

"Who d'you think he'll choose?" Colt muttered so low only Hunt would be able to hear.

"Not sure. Sloan's itching for it, though."

Colt chuckled. "I think he's wound a little tight after listening to you and your Omega."

Snorting, Hunt folded his arms over his chest, watching the pup make his mental calculations and sizing up his new Packmates. Colt's side-eyed regard caught Hunt's attention, and he jerked his chin in question.

Colt grinned. "After all this time, you found yourself an Omega, huh?"

An involuntary swell of pride puffed his chest, and Hunt huffed bitterly. "Ain't no one more fucking surprised than me, that's for damn sure. You know I wasn't looking."

"Eh…" Colt shrugged. "You couldn't stop it, even if you tried. That shit's biological." He sighed. "Count yourself lucky, Alpha. You've given me some hope that maybe it's never too late."

Hunt popped a brow. "You saying I'm old?"

"It's true whether I say it or not." Colt's mouth tipped in a teasing grin, and Hunt answered with one of his own.

A good Second and a good friend, Hunt would take razzing from Colt he'd never accept from anyone else. At almost forty years old, it was no secret Colt had been aching for an Omega for years. When they'd turned up a few on this trip, Hunt had held his breath that one of them would gravitate to Colt, but it hadn't happened. He almost felt guilty for finding Kess, but a bolt of pure, possessive ire put that emotion to rest. She was his and his alone.

Hunt turned back to the see the pup focus in on Sloan—fucking Sloan—and chuckled to himself. Sloan, as much as he was an obnoxious, loud-mouthed motherfucker, was also one of the bigger Alphas in their Pack.

The kid had guts, he'd give him that.

"You've got a big enough mouth," Heck said slowly, deliberately. "Should be a nice, fat target for my fist." He lifted an insolent shoulder. "Or my dick."

"Oh hell." Colt's voice dripped with indulgent respect.

Snickers and whoops came from the group as a slow, acidic smile spread over Sloan's coarse features. Off came Sloan's jacket and his shirt, displaying a chest like a side of beef. The pup stripped down to his waist before moving into the center of the ring and adopting a rudimentary fighting stance. Probably no one had ever taught him shit about fighting. The Pack would remedy that soon enough.

The two Alphas stalked each other, circling and sizing up, waiting to see who would strike first. The difference in size between the two bordered on comical: Sloan massive but gleeful, Heck scrawny but brave. Sloan faked a few twitches and laughed like a maniac when the kid reacted with a flinch. Impatient, he didn't wait for the laughs to die down before crossing the space and throwing a punch to the pup's ribs.

And then the fight was on. Their favorite form of entertainment, the Pack cheered and winced, laughed and taunted from the sidelines. The pup held his own, managing to land a few blows to Sloan's impenetrable abdomen and a lucky shot to his chin that only made Sloan grin wider.

Something delicious wafted across Hunt's nose, his body reacting before his mind caught up. He pitched a look over his shoulder to see Kess striding up in yesterday's clothes, her face tight and unhappy. Hunt adjusted his stance to make her space between himself and Colt and pulled her into his side, bad temper rolling off her.

"What is this?" she hissed.

Hunt lifted a brow. "Didn't your former Pack fight for membership?"

"Well, yes, but—" She cut off her own words, her eyes large and brimming with concern for the now-bloodied pup. "He's a boy."

"He's an Alpha," Colt corrected.

Sloan landed another sharp blow to the pup's face, one that sent him staggering back several steps and spitting a mouthful of blood. Kess gasped in horror, and Hunt rubbed a soothing hand up and down her thin (too thin) arm. Once this was over, he needed to get some food into her.

"Are we sure he's Alpha?" Sloan sneered from the middle of the ring. "Had a juicy Omega right under his nose and didn't even know, did he?"

"You fucker!" Heck yelled, launching himself at Sloan in a passionate, but ill-timed and sloppy attack. Sloan anticipated it, pressing his advantage, knocking blow after blow and pounding the pup's face into a swollen pulp.

Kess hid her face in her palms. "When's it over?"

"Soon, baby." Hunt kissed the top of her head, his lips brushing her cloud-soft hair. "Soon."

She whimpered, flinching at every landed blow, every wet-sounding smack, and every grunt of pain from the pup. Hunt would give the pup credit—he was taking a good beating. A punch connected with his jaw, and Heck hit the ground, groaning in pain. He held up a palm toward his tormentor.

"Yield," he said through thick lips. "I yield." He rolled onto his side, shuddering.

The fight stopped, Sloan swiping away a string of blood at the corner of his mouth, his only visible injury. He stalked toward the pup and offered him a hand up, which Heck used to stagger to his feet, all the more awkward after the righteous ass-kicking he'd received. The rest of the Pack circled in, welcoming Heck with back slaps and shoulder grabs, everyone in high spirits after starting the morning with bloodshed. The fucking animals.

Kess unburied her face and stared, horrified at the pup's injuries. "Can I help—"

"No." Hunt's anger flared that she'd even consider doting on another Alpha, pup or no. At the hurt in her eyes, he softened his tone and cupped her warm, rounded cheek in his palm. She was a teacher, the woman said, right? She'd probably taught Heck in her classroom. It would be natural for her to want to help him. He wouldn't let her, but he remembered the impulse.

Once upon a time, he'd liked to help people too.

"No, baby," he purred. "It won't help him to have you make a fuss. Would just undermine the respect he earned by taking his beating. Understand?"

She nodded. Her eyes, full of sadness, sank to the ground.

"C'mon," he said, turning her around. "Let's get you some breakfast."

CHAPTER 9

Kess

Somehow she'd forgotten the gruesome reality of the Alpha initiation ritual—or perhaps she had been shamefully less affected by it, having never had a personal connection to a fresh pup getting his inaugural beatdown. Witnessing that monster Alpha beat the snot out of the sweet, shy boy from the village had turned her stomach. What else had she forgotten, willfully or otherwise, from her time with a Pack? A weighty ball dropped in her stomach. Her immediate future promised more harsh reminders.

She stared at the bowl of food Hunter had placed in her hands with no appetite whatsoever. He'd deposited her on a rock next to the firepit, handed her the bowl with a command to eat, then disappeared into the camp. Swirling a spoon through the thick sludge dotted with bits of root vegetables, she brought a testing bite to her lips, abashed at her hesitancy to eat after so many years of hunger. Maybe it was the fight, or the sights and smells and sounds of the Alphas swarming around the camp. They snuck her quick looks as they attended to the breaking down process, but none engaged any further than a furtive, tight nod. She searched their numbers, seeking Heck's battered and bloody, but familiar face. But he was nowhere to be found, and she prayed he was off somewhere tending to his wounds.

"You better eat that before he comes back, Omega." An Alpha crouched at her side a respectful distance away. Handsome, his shaggy black hair framed hazel eyes as sharp as his jawline. She recognized him from the fight, standing next to Hunter. "I'm Colt, Hunter's Second."

She swallowed a tepid bite. The sludge was bland and inoffensive, except for the small vegetable bits that added some sweetness.

"That means you're allowed to talk to me?"

He studied her with a neutral curiosity for a beat too long, as if deciding what to make of her. She met his regard with a bland, insolent look. After what she'd witnessed— along with the complete and total upheaval of her life in a matter of hours—she wanted nothing to do with any of them.

Even worse, she wanted nothing to do with herself. The morning's activities (and the prior night's) highlighted the abrupt change in her fortunes. The day before, she'd awoken the village teacher, with a job and a purpose and a small life of her own determination. Sure, it wasn't perfect, but to see everything she'd worked for derailed and dismissed by one Alpha's whims burned. *Get up*, he'd said. And she had. *Get dressed*, he'd said. And she had. *Eat*, he'd said. And she'd eaten. *Get my cock out*, he'd said. And she had—gladly.

Shame thickened the mealy mush, and she gagged around the mouthful, another reminder of last night's activities. Enclosed and sheltered in the tent with Hunter, she'd abandoned her resolve and given over to the inevitable, allowing him to arrange and use her body as he saw fit and wallowing in every brutal second. He'd fucked her mouth full and deep, and she didn't merely tolerate it; she *relished* it. Her base Omega nature singing with delight, the experience humiliatingly marred by the unassuaged emptiness in her core. She'd endeavored to hold herself aloof, to maintain a semblance of reserve and resistance. Only to utterly fail.

Not just fail, but fail in such a spectacular, explosive fashion that the entire Alpha camp—and likely the Beta village—had heard her lusty cries. Certainly this Alpha, Colt, with his twinkling eyes, took every overheard sigh and moan as evidence of a truly contented Omega who wanted nothing more than to be fucked full of Alpha until she couldn't stand.

"Allowed?" A grin split his face like a knife, all white teeth and bronzed skin. He angled his head toward the others. "They can talk to you all they want. Nobody better touch you, though, if they know what's good for them." He paused to rearrange his long limbs, stretching his legs alongside the dying fire and crossing his ankles. "So you know the pup?"

She nodded and scooped another spoonful.

Undeterred by her sullen response, he continued, "Pretty dangerous for an unmated Omega in the midst of a bunch of Bible-y Betas, isn't it?"

"They were kind to me." She ignored the memory of her empty food donation box and swallowed another gulp.

Any amusement fell from his face. "They didn't know you."

"And you do? And he does? The only thing Alphas know is how to take whatever they want and destroy it." Her words spewed forth, bitter, but true.

Colt's eyes narrowed at her outburst, but he otherwise appeared unperturbed. "Nobody's gonna be destroying nothing having to do with you, Omega. Hunt's a good Alpha; he'll take care of you."

She snorted and shoved a bite into her mouth. "That's what the last one said," she said around the sticky glob.

Colt had no response to that. The weight of his stare pressed down on her, and she felt him studying, studying, studying. Ignoring him, she finished off the breakfast, scraping the bowl so clean it looked as if it hadn't been used.

"You want some more?" he asked.

"No, thank you."

He offered a palm and took her bowl, rising without another word. Thirsty, she picked her way over to the creek to wash her face and hands and scoop a few handfuls of cool water into her mouth. Behind her, preparation for the imminent departure wrapped up, and the group jittered with ready-to-go energy. Dangling her fingertips in the water, she said a silent goodbye to the creek and the village, pushing down mad urges to take off and make a run for it. Escape dangled like a fat worm before a hungry fish, tantalizing and oh-so-close. She knew these woods a little bit; might she use her familiarity to evade capture?

The question rang false, even in her own head. He'd track her down without a second thought. It'd be easy for him, and there'd be hell to pay afterward. At best, he'd chase her to the ground and claim her on the spot. She suppressed a loathsome shiver at the carnal thought. At worst... who knew what he'd do to secure his rebellious Omega?

His Omega. Was she his? He'd said as much, yet he hadn't claimed her when he'd had the chance. It was not clear why he'd stopped short, but she'd learn soon enough what kind of an Alpha he was. His tendencies and peculiarities and proclivities. Just as she'd learned Brock and all his myriad ways. If he was anything like her former Alpha, he'd demand an unrelenting devotion of study to him and him alone, to the exclusion of all else and regardless of her interests and wants.

Would he want pups, as Brock had? Would he become deranged if she failed to produce them, as Brock had? Would he lock her up, secluded and alone, cycle after cycle? Her hands clenched into tight, stubborn fists. That, above all, she couldn't bear. Five years out from under an Alpha's thumb, choosing her own path forward—even if her choices were often limited—had changed her. She simply couldn't go back. She wouldn't.

"You ready to go Omeg—Kess?"

She startled at the already-familiar voice, hunching her shoulders as if to conceal her thoughts at the unexpected interruption.

She tipped her head back to see his face. Lit by sunlight, the silver strands of his hair caught the sun's rays and bounced them back, like a playful game of pitch and catch. After having now seen his entire Pack in the light of day, she could, without a doubt, conclude Hunter to be not only the most imposing, but also the most exquisite. His brutal beauty derailed her seditious thoughts. Her heart beat faster in her chest, not from fear, but from her body's stirring interest.

Pushing the urges aside, she stood slowly, wiping her fingertips on her pants. "Where are we going?"

"First, swing by the village to pick up the pup." He continued at her confused expression. "He went to say goodbye to his folks. And then we head north, back to our settlement. I have a small place. I think you'll like it."

She pictured Brock's dwelling, the four walls she'd stared at for years in unending boredom. Never good at controlling her emotions, her face folded into a scowl, which Hunter noted with a half-hearted shoulder lift.

"Or you'll learn to, I suppose."

He turned to leave, silently communicating that he expected her to follow. All the Alphas waited by enormous snorting, twitching horses loaded up with their supplies. Someone handed Hunt the reins of a huge animal and, with a quick whistle, he signaled everyone to move out. Not sure exactly where to go, Kess walked beside him, noting her small pack secured to the horse's haunches.

Within minutes, the Pack entered the village clearing, embers still smoldering from last night's epic bonfire. Outside his family's dwelling, Heck hugged his younger siblings. The rest of the village stood wide-eyed in front of their shacks, holding their collective breath. Kess felt their eyes on her and color rose to her cheeks. Had they heard her orgasmic screams last night? From the scandalized looks on their faces, they had.

"You!"

Kess made eye contact with Heck's mother, a short, wiry woman who stormed over with murder in her eyes. Hunter stepped slightly in front of Kess, and the woman balked, keeping her physical distance but shooting shards of hate through her eyeballs. "This is *your* fault, you Omega *whore*. They *smelled* your disgusting cunt and came here. Did you service all of them last night? Do they take turns with you, or all at the same time?"

The contents of Kess' stomach curdled, and nausea slithered up her throat. As feared, the village had heard and, of course, they'd curse her for a whore. But not half as much as she cursed herself. If only she'd been able to rein in her Omega nature and defy Hunter's impossible pull. Worse, she'd luxuriated in it, her Omega defiant that any and all should hear her pleasure, never for one second imagining what it would be to stand before them after the fact, her own infamy on display. Her own body's betrayal stood stark and bleak in the plain light of the morning. If Hunter aimed to control her, her Omega stood at the ready to assist.

Mouth dry, her words emerged raspy and broken. "Rachel, I'm so—"

"Don't you open your filthy, cock-sucking mouth," the woman seethed, her voice cracking. "He's a good boy." She thrust a finger back toward her bruised son. "And look what *they* did to him!"

"That's enough, Beta," Hunter said, cold but firm. "The Omega had nothing to do with this. We were passing through. Now go back to your husband before you piss me off."

His words landed, and the woman wiped her brimming eyes with worn, cracked hands. Despite the attack, Kess' compassion bloomed. A mother grieving—that's all this was, no matter how nasty the words spewing out of her. A Beta mother wouldn't understand. No matter this Pack or another, Heck was always going to leave her behind. She wouldn't understand that he would make friends with his Pack brothers and not be doomed to live all his days healing from swollen eyes and bruised ribs or feeling like a giant, unwieldly monster among the Betas.

But there wasn't time to explain all that.

"I'll watch out for him, Rachel," Kess added weakly as the woman turned away.

"He doesn't need anything from you, *whore*." The woman spat over her shoulder. The tension coiling in Hunter's body scared her more than the Beta's fury. Alarmed, Kess laid a palm on his arm in gentle, instinctive assurance.

"I'll rip her to shreds if you want me to," he murmured.

Kess tightened her grip as if she'd have any chance of actually holding him back, "No. Please don't. She's losing her son, and she doesn't know what she's saying."

His eyes, silvery-blue, peered down his shoulder at her. "She doesn't deserve your pity, Kess."

Unable to look away from his icy stare, Kess swiped a thumb along the muscled grooves of his arm, finding solace in the anchoring feel of him. "Well, she's got it anyway."

His face crumpled slightly at that, as if he couldn't quite believe what he'd heard. His cheeks, scruffed and angular, melted out of the clench they'd held all morning. A rumbling purr vibrated his chest and echoed in hers, soft and meant only for her. She dropped her hand, soaking up the unexpected comfort along with his implied approval. Brock had only purred when he wanted something or to pacify her when upset. It was never for showing any kind of care or concern.

She didn't understand this Alpha.

After a moment, he stopped, and Kess cast a nervous glance around the rest of the village, driven to see who would make eye contact or wish her well. Almost no one, renewing her humiliation and chagrin. Ani's mom held her back by the shoulders, as if afraid her daughter would dart away and run close to the Alphas. They wouldn't hurt a little girl, Kess knew, but that didn't seem to matter. Kess snuck a little goodbye wave and watched Ani's big brown eyes well with tears before she turned to bury her face in her mother's leg.

Water threatened to pour from Kess' eyes in response. Whatever point the Alpha had thought he was making by bringing her here to experience this shunning, this had been her home. They don't know you, Colt had said. Yeah, well, they didn't need to, did they? There was more to her than her biology.

Unfortunately, in the AfterEnd, her biology was the only thing anyone—Alphas and Betas alike—seemed to see.

CHAPTER 10

Hunter

The horses were rested and the Alphas anxious to move, so they beat a brisk path due west. The two pack horses' loads had been rearranged so the new pup would have a mount, and he assigned Mick to keep an eye on Heck since he'd never ridden before.

Once the gasoline and oil had run out after TheEnd, Hunt learned the ins and outs of actual horsepower. Now he knew more about horses than he ever did about muscle cars. Hunt liked horses—his, in particular. He'd spent innumerable enjoyable hours plodding over terrain atop Cleo.

But none so satisfying as the last several with Kess seated between his thighs. Even with his tortured dick complaining in an ever-escalating pitch, he wouldn't give up the feel of her warm bottom snugged against him for anything.

After the scene with Heck's mom, he'd handed Kess up into the saddle. Thankfully, she'd not hesitated to climb the enormous beast. She'd sat high above the Betas, her posture straight and dignified like a fucking queen, while he led the horse beyond the village's borders. His chest warmed with pride at her refusal to accept any of the shame that wretched Beta bitch had attempted to heap on her, which helped assuage his own guilt for letting the woman's railing go on as long as he did. Already guessing her intentions toward Kess, he'd wanted to shut her up before she'd said a single hateful word, but he'd held himself back.

It pained him—no, it near-eviscerated him—to watch someone hurl insults at his Omega like that. No question. If it had been anyone other than the pup's weak, half-starved Beta mother, he'd have pounded them straight into the ground without a second thought. But he'd allowed it, if only to demonstrate to Kess how much her safety and acceptance in the village had been an illusion—a convenient illusion she'd clutched with white knuckles, but an illusion nonetheless. He'd said to her last night, *You're an Omega. Your place is with a Pack*, and he'd meant it. As much as a pain in the ass Omegas could be, they fared better when protected by a Pack than alone. Of this, he had no doubt.

He tipped forward, riffling his nose through her impossibly soft, fragrant curls, and was rewarded as an appreciative shiver washed down her back.

"We won't stop till sundown, but if you need to relieve yourself, you tell me," he said in her ear, wanting to break the ice after hours of silence.

A single nod was her only response. She stared straight ahead at the overgrown trail as they picked their way through the wilderness. It made sense to follow the creek as it headed west, same as them. He suspected it would grow and empty to a sizeable river before flowing all the way to the coast. The Columbian, perhaps? Between the bombs, the earthquakes, the volcanos, and the fires, so much of the landscape had been changed and rearranged in the years since TheEnd. Coupled with his fallible memory, nothing was ever where he expected it to be. At times, his waking life resembled the hazy familiarity of a half-remembered dream.

A gust of wind stirred Kess' hair and blasted a fresh burst of her delicious scent into his face, dispelling all concerns about geography. She, at least, was real, an answer to an unspoken prayer. He grunted low and involuntarily tightened his arms round the Omega. She sucked a sharp breath, her breasts lifting above his arm, and his next inhale brought the sweet flavor of slick to his awareness. His Omega feigned indifference, but her body betrayed her.

"Or," he said, his voice coarse and gravelly, "if you need me to relieve something else for you…" Hunt dragged the tip of his nose behind the delicate curl of her ear, the slight touch stiffening her body with arousal and hunger. "Did you enjoy last night?"

"Yes, but—" A breath shuddered and rocked over her shoulders. "Why… Why didn't…?" Her words trailed away as if she couldn't bring herself to say them out loud. But he knew what she was asking. Why hadn't he taken her fully? Claimed her for himself and placed a mating bite?

He passed a thumb over her thick nipple, unable to stop himself from toying with the jutting nub. Dainty shivers rolled down her spine, and Hunt smiled to himself. So much to explore on this lush little Omega. He'd barely scratched the surface.

"Are you disappointed?" Amusement tinged his tone. "The tent is barely big enough for me," he explained, sweeping his thumb over her beaded tip. Such a small touch, yet it wound her up with every swipe. The air between her spread thighs thickened with the scent of slick. "I want to take you where I can see you, stretched out in the sunlight, on a blanket big enough to move around without worry we'll pull the tent down on top of us. Should we stop now, d'you think? Cut away from the Pack and take care of this?"

He punctuated the question with a sharp nipple pinch, and she whimpered in his arms.

"Is that a yes?" he asked, snaking a hand down her stomach and teasing his fingers over her sex. Legs spread over Cleo's wide back, her body was swollen and humid there, her threadbare pants sodden with arousal.

"What do you care?" she forced out throatily. "Won't you just take what you want whenever you want it?"

His hand paused in its casual toying, her words reeking of judgement and low expectations. Hunter didn't care for it one bit. Ignoring his body's demands, he withdrew his playful touches and adjusted the reins. This Omega lumped him in with the monsters of her last Pack, and he wasn't having it. He didn't know what she'd gone through, but given the marks on her shoulders, it hadn't been pleasant. He had sympathy for her, and no shortage of anger for the last bastard who had abused her perfect body, but hadn't he showed he wouldn't hurt her?

He'd been nothing but the picture of restraint and accommodation since first laying eyes on her, huddled in her decaying shack. God knew his instincts screamed at him to drag her to camp and fuck her next to the fire for anyone who wanted to fill their eyes and know she belonged to him.

He hadn't, though. Didn't he deserve some credit for that?

Shifting uncomfortably around his throbbing dick, he swung a glance backward down the line of Alphas on horseback, wishing he had someone to ask about this. Having never paid much attention to the courting rituals— if you could call them that—of other Alpha-Omega pairs, Hunter found himself at a loss as to how to proceed with this one. Like she'd said, his nature, his body, and his very essence commanded him to take, take, take.

But her words held him back. That was exactly what she'd accused Alphas of doing—taking without regard to anything or anyone else. And maybe if he'd been born an Alpha and had never known another way of living, like Colt or all these other fuckers, he'd be okay with that. Yet he hadn't always been like this.

That old, smothered part of him agreed with the Omega, and felt disgusted by his urges too.

"All right, Omega, you don't want me to take? That's no problem," he said through gritted teeth, not entirely believing the promise he was about to make. "How about this—you let me know when you need what I can give you, yeah? When you can't wait another single minute, another second, for me to ease that ache between your thighs. When the thought of going without makes you feel like you're losing your stubborn mind, you go on ahead and let me know."

Her breath whooshed out in an agonized staccato. "You're talking about a Heat, and I don't have those anymore."

"Am I?" he challenged. "I guess we'll see. Because my prediction is, Heat or no Heat, you'll be begging me soon enough."

Christ, he hoped so. The taunts fell off his tongue, bolstered by his frustration and irritation. This was just more evidence that all the talk about the sacred Alpha-Omega bond was as much a bunch of bullshit as he'd always suspected. Here he was, Alpha of Alphas of this strong Pack, having to goad a truculent Omega into climbing on his cock.

This wasn't the way this was supposed to go. *Fuck.* What a mess. And what the hell did she mean, she didn't have Heats anymore? Was she in some sort of Omega menopause? What the fuck was that? And what if she did go into Heat and resisted him despite it?

Anxiety dug its bony fingertips under his bravado. He'd seen Omegas lose their fucking minds if they refused to relieve their Heat urges. The vision of Kess rolling around, sweating and sticky and coated in slick, her pelvis pumping into the air as she groaned and cried and ranted in frustration, gouged a path straight through his mind. Decades ago, he'd witnessed a stubborn Omega snarl and fight and scream, scratching and biting any Alpha who approached, determined not to succumb.

The Pack had lost its mind in concert with her display. Fights had broken out, the Alphas near-rabid in the presence of the mewling, miserable Omega. Innumerable angry, shouting debates over to whether they ought to just hold her down and take her.

Hunt had held them back, fighting physically and verbally for days with his own cock aching like an itch he couldn't scratch deep in his brain, pinned by his anachronistic morals to resist forcing an unwilling Omega. But what was the moral choice when she'd die without mating?

Before TheEnd, he'd held down belligerent, out-of-their-mind patients and administered life-saving medical care, hadn't he? Wasn't this the same? It was hard to know. Hard to know what was best for the Omega, especially when what seemed best for her aligned so closely with what each Alpha wanted for themselves. Altruism or opportunism? Compassion or exploitation? Who the fuck knew?

If he'd only known what would happen, things might've gone differently. In the end, he'd fended off the would-be Alpha rapists, helped by a few like-minded peers, but had nearly been killed by the escalating violence as her Heat went on. For his efforts, the Omega, neglected for a few minutes during one of these flare-ups, escaped and drowned herself in the lake. They'd chased after her, six Alphas swimming in and searching for her body in the frigid, murky depths. But it was too late; she'd disappeared and was never seen again.

After days of whining and moaning from the Omega, pleading and snarling from the Alphas, everything had gone silent the moment she'd slipped underwater. Hunt remembered the silence that had roared in his ears, and the bone-deep knowledge he'd fucked up in an irreversible way.

Despite his promise to Kess, he flexed his hand around her waist. If anything were to happen to this one, he'd never forgive himself. He hoped to any god who was listening that it wouldn't come to that.

But if it did, he knew what he would do.

CHAPTER 11

Kess

The day dragged on and on over the endless terrain and the clop-clopping of the horses' hooves. The Alphas maintained a steady stream of rumbling conversation that didn't hold her interest. It all struck her as general masculine nonsense, nothing worth straining her ears to attend to.

Not that she would've been able to focus on anything beyond the overwhelming presence of Hunter's chest against her back, his arms around her sides, and his scent absolutely everywhere. She'd sneak deeper and deeper breaths, striving to catch any forest scent other than the loamy Alpha sharpness that permeated every inhale. But it was impossible; he was a creature of, and inseparable from, the wild, damp forest they trudged through.

Worst of all, she couldn't get away. Any attempt at shallow breathing to minimize the effects only succeeded in heightening every other touch and sensation assaulting her senses. Her body hovered on the knife's edge of insanity, worsened by his sneering certainty she would be begging for his attentions in short order.

Begging. The word filled her with ominous anticipation—a thing she both craved and despised.

Nearing dusk, the Alphas identified a suitable spot and invaded, dismounted and commenced the process of establishing camp. Without much direction from either Hunter or Colt, each Alpha set about chores and duties without complaint. Hunt slipped off the back of the horse and helped Kess down with brisk efficiency and none of the tantalizing touches and strokes from earlier in the day. Her legs wobbled under her, her thighs and rear shooting pain across her hips and pelvis from an entire day on horseback. Kess massaged her bottom, trying to restore a feeling other than numb agony.

Hunt's eyes narrowed and sparked with good humor. "You'll get used to it."

"Hopefully sooner rather than later," she muttered, taking in her surroundings. Dense forest surrounded them, not much different from the village. "How far do you think we came today?"

"Not far." Hunt removed the saddlebags from his horse, his brow gathered in thought. "Maybe twenty miles? We ought to pick up the pace tomorrow."

"You said you live to the north, so why are we heading west?"

He glanced up from unstrapping the saddle, his blue eyes betraying surprise at her interest.

"It's not a weird question," she added testily. "Can't I know?"

His expression settled, and he responded with the matter-of-factness that seemed to characterize his interactions—with other Alphas, at least. His treatment of her was decidedly more complex. "We stayed inland when we traveled south, and now we're heading west to the ocean. Then we'll turn back toward home."

"Okay." She breathed a miniscule sigh of relief. She'd traveled quite a bit after her elopement from Brock's Pack, and her knowledge of geography was limited, but she knew that pack resided to the south. There would be no danger of an accidental reunion.

Hunter quirked a brow. "That's good news?"

"Uh…" Kess rubbed at her folded arms, the falling temperature creeping through her thin clothes without the auxiliary heat provided by Hunt and the horse. "Just as long as we aren't going south."

Frowning, he dug through a pack and pulled out a blanket, draping it over her shoulders. "Your former Pack was south?"

She nodded, drawing the blanket closed over her chest. It felt good, both the blanket and the care.

An angry growl from her stomach pierced the air, and the corner of Hunt's mouth ticked up. "We'll get you fed soon, Omega."

"Alpha." A fresh-faced pup with brown skin and a scruffy beard jogged over. "I smelled some blackberries growing on the other side of the creek. Would it be all right if I take Heck and we pick some?" He snuck a shy glance at Kess. "Thought the Omega might like some fresh food."

At the mention of Heck, Kess' eyes swung around the assembling camp, searching for her former pupil. Despite the hatred from his mother, she'd made a promise to look after him and intended to keep it. Picking berries offered a perfect chance to check his injuries and chat beyond the snooping ears of the rest of the Pack. She didn't know when she'd get another chance to talk with him alone.

The thought doused her with the reality of how quickly her life had changed. Yesterday being alone with Heck in the schoolhouse had triggered a near panic, and today she angled to get him alone to talk. Only now, as much as she chafed against Hunter's possessiveness, she had to admit it afforded her a degree of protection she'd lacked for a long time. Colt had affirmed as much at the fire that morning—no other Alphas would interfere with their leader's Omega.

Kess turned toward Hunter. "I can help. I'd like to."

"No," the two Alphas responded at the same time, and Kess startled at their unexpected vehemence. The pup flashed her an apologetic look, but deferred to Hunt with a diminutive chin tuck. Hunt merely went back to his unloading without providing any explanation, unaware—or unconcerned—that any of her fledgling positive feelings about him had evaporated.

Chastised, Kess pressed her lips together, seething. What the hell did he think was going to happen to her? She'd assumed the two Alpha pups would come along. What kind of danger could she be in with them around? What was she supposed to do, stand around like a lump while the Pack made camp? Wait patiently to be fed and bedded and fucked for all to hear?

Hunt cleared his throat. "Don't want you out of my sight," he said as if that were an explanation. "Go on, Alek. Finish tending to the horses, then take the new pup. Stay together."

With a shy nod, the pup Alek darted away. Hunt retrieved a brush and began wiping down his horse without another word.

Fine. Kess whirled and marched toward the small fire an Alpha stoked in the middle of the camp. There were other places for her to be in his precious sight without being anywhere near him.

"Omega!" Hunter's sharp voice cut across the camp, but Kess grit her teeth and ignored him. Alphas' eyes followed her, brimming with curiosity at the sign of friction, but she didn't give one single fuck, plopping down beside the fire in a huff and tucking the blanket around her legs.

She hated this. Years hiding in the Beta village, blending into the background and keeping a low profile, only to come full circle and be unable to do something as simple as pick berries without an Alpha's permission. She stared into the fire, refusing to betray any interest in the Pack whatsoever.

As if sensing her black mood, all of the Alphas' genial interactions dwindled, and she could make out only hushed, businesslike mutterings.

Her stomach growled again, louder in the tense hush of the camp. Hunter passed by without a word and dropped a pouch into her lap. Her eyes never left the fire, but she identified his scent as it whispered across her nose, coming close and then retreating as he barked orders to the sullen Alphas.

With impatient fingers she jerked open the pouch, sniffing at the dried meat and fruit inside. Lamenting her lack of fortitude, her inability to resist, she fished pieces of meat out and shoved them into her mouth. Chewy, tough, and highly salted, the flavor soaked her tongue and brought saliva rushing to her cheeks. The first few bites settled her stomach and immediately improved her mood. Hunger having been a persistent presence in her life, she no longer recognized her body's signal for food. It had become the sensation of existence, of being awake, of being alive. Satiation had become a novelty.

She shoveled the rations in her mouth, chewing and chewing and chewing, letting the monotony lull her into calm. Her whirling emotions stilled, and the conversations of the Alphas picked up around her. They peppered Hunter and Colt with questions and became embroiled in some discussion around mending a fraying bridle and some spoilt food.

Belly full and warmed from the fire, Kess' mouth demanded water. Feeling deviant, she rose from the firepit and headed for the creek, pointedly not making eye contact with anyone or asking for permission. If he wanted to keep her in eyeshot, he could damned well follow.

She wove through the woods, tracking the sound of the bubbling creek beyond a copse of trees. The horses scattered around the green banks on either side, loosely tethered and munching on fresh spring grass. A few whinnied as she passed by, and she gave an affectionate stroke here and there, breathing a sigh of relief no one had stopped her. Maybe she could steal a few minutes and wash the travel grime and the Alpha scent off her body.

Kneeling to drink, she glanced around and sniffed the air for any sign of Hunter. A self-satisfied smile tickled her lips when she caught neither sight nor smell of the obnoxious Alpha. How she'd managed to slip away without notice, she had no idea, but it felt good all the same. The dark woods beckoned in front of her, luring her to keep going and run, to escape.

If only it were that simple.

Brock's unexpected death had seemed too good to be true. She'd longed for escape for so long, yet had never dreamed she'd have an actual chance. But when the moment came, a plan materialized almost immediately. She'd feign a mourning period and steal away under their notice, disguising her scent so as not to be followed. Packing what she needed for survival and as many provisions as she could carry, she'd set out with determination and a vague plan to head north.

She had none of that now. As Hunter had rightly noted, her clothes were worn, her boots were falling apart, and she didn't have even a spare piece of jerky to her name. She could run, but she wouldn't get far.

Shaking her head, she laid out her blanket and pulled off her shirt. Her breasts pebbled with gooseflesh and her nipples pinched as she splashed the frigid, barely thawed water on her chest and shoulders. Scrubbing briskly under her arms and over the area where he'd spilled his seed, she bathed as best as she could without soap or a cloth. Handful after determined handful, she slapped water on her skin and sluiced it off. The chill bit into her all the way to her bones, but she grit her teeth against it. She wanted this Alpha *off* of her.

She bent for another handful, and a hand sealed across her mouth, smothering her shriek. The next instant she was facedown on the blanket, crushed by a huge Alpha body of an entirely different scent than the one she had cleansed away. Fear swelled in her throat.

No. Not like this. Not again.

Massive hips and thighs restricted her movements, and her attempt to buck him off was met with a dark, cruel chuckle. Alpha mass plastered to her back, shoulders pinned by his chest, her arms uselessly flapped backward, grabbing and scratching at anything but getting nowhere.

"Sweet, trusting Omega," he crooned in her ear, so quiet she wondered if he was inside her head. "Maybe Hunter's too much of a pussy to give you what you need, but I'm sure as fuck not."

After some rustling and shifting, the night air clawed at her exposed buttocks. He growled, a sharp, demanding noise, and her Omega body responded, soaking her in slick despite her utter terror. She didn't want this. She screamed behind his paw, snapping and biting, and earned herself a sharp, painful strike on her hip.

"Shut the fuck up, Omega whore," he swore, yanking her head back and stretching her neck to the point of pain. Her eyes wrenched open wide, circling the woods for any help, but only the horses stared back, placidly munching. "Hold still while I take your cunt. If you piss me off, I'll knot your tight little ass too, and believe me, you will *not* like that." He chuckled again. "Not as much as I would, that's for sure."

As if to emphasize his intent, a hard, angry cock drooled on the back of her thigh. Kess whimpered, every muscle in her body locking up from cold and fright. Just last night, she'd been drunk on Hunter's cock, but this foreign one, rife with violence and exigence, made a mockery of those lusty moments. Pleading words spilled from her captured mouth as he kneed her thighs apart.

"Shut *up*," he growled again as he shoved rough fingers into her dripping body. "You're gonna like this, Omega, you'll see. I'm going to knot you and mark you, and that pussy Hunt won't be able to do a motherfucking thing about it."

Tears raced down her face, and she knew he told the vulgar, brutal truth. Oh God. She'd thought she'd come full circle before, but she was wrong. This was full circle— being mounted in the woods on a dirty blanket by an Alpha whose face she couldn't even see. How could she have ever thought she'd escaped Brock? He was still here. He was everywhere.

She'd never be free.

CHAPTER 12

Hunter

In the end, only two bags of oats were growing the fuzzy green mold. Would've been nice to know who let the bags get wet without spreading the grains out to dry, but he doubted anyone would bother to fess up. It wouldn't salvage anything, anyway.

"Well, guess we'll be doing a bit more hunting on the way back home." Colt sighed, sifting the ruined grains through his fingers.

"Not great for the GI sys—"

Male shouts burst through the quiet forest. Hunt's eyes swung to the fire, where he'd left Kess with a pre-dinner snack. Alarm rocketed up his spine.

She wasn't there.

In a blink, Hunt tore across the woods in the direction of the shouts, followed by Colt and the rest of the Pack on his heels. His nostrils flared, seeking her scent and catching it, ripe with slick and overlaid with fear. Another scent poisoned the air—lust-ridden Alpha stink. *Oh no. Oh fuck, no.* His feet sped across the rugged terrain, barely touching the ground as they ate up the distance.

Horses whinnied and scattered, jittery with the smell of Alpha violence, adding to the chaos. The banks of the creek cleared, and the horror came into focus. Kess, half-naked, her pants around her knees, crawled away from the water, sobs ripping from her lungs. Van, pants undone and dangling open, lunged and punched at Alek and Heck, their faces already bloodied as the bigger Alpha dominated the fight.

Violence blazed through Hunter's body, hot and immediate.

"You *motherfucker*," Hunt snarled, tackling Van backward into the water. "What did you do to her?"

"What you wouldn't." Van smacked his forehead into Hunt's nose. Hunter's head jerked back, pain knocking on his senses, but he refused to answer, returning the blow with his own skull. Undiluted wrath bubbled up and flowed through his veins. He landed a punch to Van's face, then another.

Van, a large Alpha, absorbed them and returned a blow, knocking Hunt off-center and pitching him to the side. He rolled with the motion and was on his feet, catching the sight of Van's still-hard cock jutting from his open pants. Fury shot through the top of his head, and he launched again, one thought searing through the rage. *He hurt the Omega. He hurt my Omega.*

One sentence unlocked a stockpile of strength years of Alpha challenges had never touched. It lived in his muscles, lodged between the twisting fibers, summoned into existence by this insult, this injury to a single Omega. Hunt's body would not stop. He wasn't Hunt anymore; he was rage itself.

Launching himself again, he plowed into Van's body with the full force of his anger. Hands scrabbling at Van's shirt, he slammed the Alpha's head down into rocky creek bed. Thick-skulled and solid, Van blinked once before locking his palms around Hunt's neck, squeezing to cut off his wind and blood. Stars blinked in Hunt's vision, but he persisted, striking Van's head to the ground again.

Van held tight. Hunt's vision narrowed as he fought the strangling, clawing at the other Alpha's tightly wrapped paws. Not caring about anything—not honor, not respect, not anything but destruction—he turned and buried an elbow between Van's legs. The first blow elicited a pained grunt, but the second, third, and fourth loosened the vise-like grip around his neck. Blood roared back into Hunt's face, and fresh air whooshed into his lungs.

Vision cleared, he spotted the sharp edge of a rock jutting to his left, its shadow menacing. *He hurt the Omega. He hurt* my *Omega,* chanted in his head, and, in one swift move, he hauled Van's massive body two feet to the left and slammed his temple into the jagged shard. Van's hands fluttered, grasping again for Hunt's neck, but they never reached their target. Again, again, again, Hunter pounded Van's thick skull against the rock. Bones cracked and shifted and ground under his hands, appalling, disgusting sensations he barely registered.

Van's face slackened as the fight drained from his limbs. With a flip, Hunt forced Van's destroyed face into the water, holding him under for his final soggy breaths.

Blood running into his eyes, Hunt pinned the dead Alpha for he didn't know how long, refusing to let go lest the motherfucker somehow come back to life and threaten Kess again.

"Alpha," a cautious voice said to his right. "Alpha, he's dead. You can let go."

Hunt knew the voice. It was Colt. His brother. His friend.

Rage cleared from his vision, and he came back to himself, taking in the rest of the solemn Pack cluttering the creek. He scanned the crowd and saw only Alpha faces, some shocked, some satisfied, some horrified.

"Where is she?" Hunt screamed, heaving himself upright. His head circled so fast dizziness threatened to swipe him off his feet. "Where's my Omega?"

CHAPTER 13

Kess

Kess ran. As soon as the two pups appeared and knocked her attacker off her back, she crawled to her feet and ran. Yanking her pants up her hips and dragging the blanket behind her, she ran, breasts bouncing painfully as she hurled herself into the dark forest.

She could smell him. Smell his acrid palm sweat smeared over her nose and mouth. She could taste him on her tongue, and her stomach recoiled. Directionless, she tore off, heading away from the screams and the Alpha howls of violence behind her. Her attacker would kill those pups. He would smash their heads together, then he would find her and finish what he'd started. Impale her on his slimy erection in every hole until she couldn't remember a time she knew anything other than his invasion.

Sobs choked her throat, and she tripped and fell, smacking her palms on rough tree roots. Moonlight abandoned her here, and she could barely see a yard beyond. But it didn't matter. Righting herself, she stumbled forward and heard the footsteps behind. Heard the rough breathing.

He was here. He'd found her, and she'd run where no one help would be coming. Thoughts piled up. Should she yell, or would that give her location away? Could he see her with his Alpha vision? This would be a game to him. A hunter and prey.

Hunter.

It wasn't Hunter behind her. She would know.

Kess lurched forward and she tripped again, scraping her forearms and slicing her breasts on the uneven terrain. She howled in pain, making a beacon of herself in the silent woods. If an Alpha didn't find her, a wolf surely would.

"Miz Kess," a gentle voice called. "Miz Kess, stop running, *please*. You're gonna hurt yourself."

No more than ten feet away was another Alpha. Closer than she'd thought. Lying prone on the ground, Kess buried her face in her bleeding arms and sobbed. Now he'd rape her here in the dirt, her face abraded by roots and bark, and no one to hear her scream.

"Miz Kess, it's me, Heck," the voice spoke louder, rising above her wrenching sobs. "I'm not gonna hurt you."

A part of her recognized the voice, the name, and the faint, warm memories associated with it, but another part screamed even louder. He was an Alpha, he knew, the Betas would know, she wasn't safe in the village, they'd cast her out. The quaking came from deep inside. From a place threatened yet untouched by her attacker. Her cries wouldn't stop. They grated her throat raw, then scraped over the rawness.

"Miz Kess, *please* stop crying. I'm not gonna hurt you, I swear," he pleaded. An object thudded next to her.

"That's water, have some water. I won't come any closer, okay? I'll stay over here."

He wasn't lying. He stayed away, standing in the shadow of an enormous tree, maybe the one whose roots had felled her. Alpha scent pinged her nose, but no lust colored its green and verdant notes. Clean and fresh like a spring sapling, it soothed her in a wholesome, natural way.

In the hushed forest, the Alpha offered a hesitant, stuttering purr. Perhaps the first he'd ever attempted. It paled in comparison to the rich timbre of Hunter's resonant rumble, but it provided something for her to focus on outside of her shredded psyche. She accepted the peaceful lull it promised and let her shoulders still from their wretched heaving.

"Alpha of Alphas." The young Alpha's purr ceased, and new Alpha scents assailed her.

They'd found her. With their sharp Alpha eyes, they'd see her right in front of them. And smell her. Kess hunched further into her arms, cold with the knowledge she'd never be able to hide.

"What did you do?" a lethal voice snarled.

A thudding impact and a sharp *oof* came from behind her. "I didn't touch her, Alpha," the pup gasped as if something—or someone—squeezed his throat. "I followed her to make sure she was all right. She fell there. I haven't touched her, I swear."

"Leave us." A grunt, then a sliding slump, followed by retreating footsteps.

The Alpha prowled closer, and a familiar sharp, woodsy scent pierced her nose, complicated by the metallic tang of blood and death. Warmth enveloped her shoulder, a solid, comforting touch, yet her body flinched from it, grinding more dirt and debris into her wounds.

"Get up," he ordered. "You're gonna freeze to death."

As if by his command, the cold permeated her awareness. She was shaking. She hadn't noticed. Muscles locked so tight they vibrated, she felt no cold, she felt nothing. Blissful, comforting void. Even his Alpha presence didn't frighten her now.

He might hurt her, he might not. All of it was beyond her control.

"Omega... *Kess*..." His gruff tone rolled over her like a leaf floating over rocks in the creek. "C'mon, get up."

With this last instruction, he hauled her up to sitting. Upright now, tears and snot dribbled down her face, all of it instantly sticky and chilled in the night air. His shadow crouched close to the ground, faint beams of moonlight snagging on his silver hair. Silver. *Hunter's* silver hair. Mesmerized, she stared at those delicate tendrils as if she could follow them straight out of this horrid world and into another.

"What the fuck were you doing by the creek?" he bit out. Faintly, like a wolf howling in the distance, she became aware of his seething anger. Aware of it as an idea, a thought. She knew it was there, yet its caged menace failed to touch her.

Kess' eyes traced his silver threads like a curving trail of stars, remembering a version of herself that marked them as beautiful. "I was thirsty."

"I told you to stay where I could see you. D'you think I said that for *my* benefit? You could've... he could've... *Fuck*!"

The Alpha, Hunter, shot to his feet, taking his star-touched hair with him. He paced away, snorting and huffing, running his hands over his head, his agitation seeming to grow with each short circuit in front of her.

"Alpha," a soft voice said in the darkness. Colt, her brain supplied when he stepped into the meager light. He carried a pack and some bowls with wisps of steam snaking upward. "Food and your tent. Thought you might want to stay here rather than come back to camp." He offered the items to Hunter, who made no move to take them, his agitated hands pawing at his head as if he had forgotten how to do something as mundane as accept a plate of food. Colt set the items down on a rock and stood. "Want me to make you a fire?"

This seemed to shake Hunter from his stupor, and he grunted a no. With a sharp nod, Colt disappeared back into the darkness, and they were once again alone.

Stirred into action, Hunt retrieved the blanket from where she had dropped it in her series of falls. After a snap to clear it of debris, he dropped it in her lap without any of the tenderness with which he'd wrapped her in it earlier.

CHAPTER 14

Hunter

Endorphins roaring through his body, Hunt stalked the area where the Omega had fallen. After disposing of Van, he'd tracked her, dodging the trees like a madman, following the fear-poisoned Omega scent. He'd picked up the young Alpha's musk and it drove him faster, a fear he hadn't considered compelling him forward. What if she'd escaped Van, only to be hunted down by another?

He'd kill them all.

His entire Pack would die by his hands, and it would be a fucking delight.

But the pup waited nearby, a respectful distance away. It was the pup from her village, and Hunt had detected no lie on him when he explained he had followed her for protection. Hunt would thank him later, once he had working brain cells again.

His body, revved and thrumming, demanded one of two things, and he'd already killed someone tonight. With a frustrated growl, Hunt began to gather wood, armful after armful, and dumped it in a pile. The Omega hadn't moved except to arrange the blanket to cover her nakedness. Blood-tinged air surrounded her, but even with his Alpha sight, he couldn't catalog her injuries in the pitch-black forest. It hadn't escaped his notice that she was shirtless.

Fucking unmated Omegas. Always, universally, unequivocally a fucking problem.

This was his fault. He ought've pulled her off the horse and claimed her in the woods today. He ought've done it last night, instead of being greedy and waiting for some pre-apocalyptic romantic notion of sunlight and blankets and enthusiastic consent. He ought've done it when she'd rocked that lush ass against him all afternoon, slowly driving him insane. Instead he'd taunted her with her own lust, teased her about begging to be fucked, and left her open to disaster.

Stooping, Hunt piled the wood and pulled the fire-starter kit from his pocket. With practiced movements honed over a century of making fires, he managed a decent flame in short order.

"Omega, come warm yourself."

She didn't stir from where she huddled on the ground, staring at nothing. With an irritated sigh, Hunt gathered the inert Omega in his arms. No protest graced her lips, and for once, he wished for her embittered griping. Some evidence her spirit remained untouched.

Settling her by the growing fire, he pushed the cooled food into her hands.

Adrenalin still cycled in his arteries, but was no longer pumping out of his adrenals. The waning surge left him rattled and queasy. Nonetheless, he forced a few spoons of the stew in his mouth, if only to give himself something to do. He tasted nothing.

Unable to sit still, he turned his focus to setting up his tent. Challenging to find a flat, dry spot near the fire in the absolute dark, but he managed, checking every few minutes on the inert Omega. Once all the blankets had been fluffed, arranged, then fluffed and arranged again, Hunt knew he'd waited long enough.

She didn't react to his approach—not a single muscle twitch or eyelash flicker. Instincts warred within him. His Alpha screamed to mate her and be done with it. It flared with the argument of inevitability. But his residual human protested. She was too fragile; she'd endured an assault. She was in shock. His Alpha did not care, arguing the cure for an unhappy Omega would always be Alpha attention.

Hunt wasn't so sure. Not knowing what else to do, he settled himself in front of her, his legs bracketing her shivering body and his eyes trained on hers. At this, her gaze did hop to his.

"I smell him. On my skin. I need…" She swallowed. "I need it off me."

Her quiet plea curdled his stomach.

"All right." Emotion scraped his voice into something far gruffer than he wanted. It had been so long since gentleness had been required of him, he'd forgotten how to offer it. Clearing his throat, he tried again, mellowing the instinctive clip of a command. "Move closer to the fire to keep warm."

Hunt stood again, and Kess inched nearer the flames. She held up her palms to the heat, and the blanket fell off one rounded, beautiful shoulder, her scars barely visible. A vision of that shoulder mangled and bleeding with Van's fresh bite mark flashed through his mind and renewed his nausea. Peeling out of his soggy shirt, Hunt inhaled a whiff of his own intensified Alpha musk and knew what he had to do.

"It's too cold to bathe in the creek, but I'm going to clean you up as best I can, Kess."

Retrieving a nearby canteen, he eased the blanket off her shoulders. Her dirt-flecked hair was soft in his fingers as he corralled it in a gentle fist. Van's sour Alpha attar rose from her skin and overwhelmed her sweet Omega scent, choking him with wrongness.

Killing Van once didn't seem nearly enough.

"This is gonna be pretty cold." Hunt tipped the canteen and drizzled water over her neck and back. She jumped and shivered at the icy touch, but didn't pull away. Working with one hand, he used his soggy shirt and scrubbed her skin. Starting high up on her neck, at her hairline, over her shoulders, and down the central planes of her back. No inch was spared. He scoured as best he could without soap, determined to wipe away all traces of Van.

Hunt worked in stony silence, shadows licking at the dense forest around them. Circling to her front, she dropped the blanket and revealed the injuries to her chest and arms. Bark, small stones, and debris clung to shallow gashes across her breasts. None actively bled, but they must've hurt. He felt a roar threatening in his throat, but he swallowed it back, focusing on the Omega.

They exchanged a quick, silent conversation of raised eyebrows and scant nods, him asking and her granting permission before he reached to cleanse her chest and breasts as best he could. He cleaned the abrasions, then worked down her arms and over her hands, removing the dirt from under her fingernails with his own.

"My face," she murmured as he massaged her roughened palms. "He…" She sucked on her lips with a grimace. "… put his hand over my mouth, and I can… *taste* him."

Wrath beat a drum against his sternum, but fury wouldn't help right now, not when he had an Omega to care for. Turning the shirt to a fresh spot, he dumped water to resoak the cloth. She held her hair out of the way, presenting her face for his attention. Here, more than anywhere else, he vowed to erase every molecule. Brows and cheeks and nose and lips and chin—all of it cleansed and purified in the firelight by his tender but thorough ministrations.

Tears balanced on her lower lids as she watched him. Her first sign of an emotion other than numbness. The first ray of hope shone through his misery. Perhaps she wasn't completely destroyed. Perhaps she'd forgive him.

"Is it gone?" Hunt asked, the cloth lingering for another pass over her upper lip and nostrils.

She nodded, eyes round and grave, her tears having retreated without spilling forth. Firelight kissed the side of her face, illuminating a rich brown eye, its pupil large with craving and glowing skin so fucking beautiful he could cry for the first time in a hundred years.

"I just smell you."

At that, his Alpha purred with satisfaction. He'd used his shirt and scented her, not only erasing any trace of the other male, but marking her as his alone.

And she knew it.

Arousal blasted through him, his body instantly hard and demanding, agonized with the pent-up need of a day of deprivation, a fierce Alpha battle, and a luscious Omega's sultry gaze.

"C'mon," he said, pulling her to her feet. "We got one last thing to take care of."

CHAPTER 15

Kess

Kess was upright, and Hunter led to the tent before a single word left her mouth. With two impatient tugs, he removed her pants and gestured her inside. Nude in a tent thick with the scented remains of what they'd done last night, she understood his agenda in no uncertain terms. Had it been only last night? A small eternity had passed since she'd come on his tongue in an unhinged fit of lust.

Shivers of uncertain origin rocked up and down her body. Excitement? Fear? Some of both? Nothing made sense. Less than an hour ago, she'd been bucking and fighting a gigantic Alpha while his dick oozed a slimy threat on the back of her leg, her body numb and distant at the impending assault.

And now? Her body vibrated in tense anticipation, half-drunk on Hunter's piney scent.

Who was this Alpha, this Hunter? She knew him not at all. Before tonight, she hadn't cared to know, content in her belief all Alphas were interchangeable. Now she wasn't so sure. He'd killed her attacker; she needed no verbal confirmation. Then, reeking of violence and death, he'd hunted her to where she lay prone and bruised on the forest floor. But... why hadn't he claimed her right then and there? She'd been present at more than one Alpha fight over an Omega; the victor mounted his prize as soon as the fight ended.

Yet Hunter hadn't. Instead he'd thrown himself into making camp, building a fire and pitching the tent, then when his attentions turned to her, he painstakingly wiped her body down and washed the attacker away. His careful touches lulled her as he'd wiped her body and cleaned her wounds like she was something delicate and precious. She'd never known an Alpha's touch to be so sweetly attentive, almost reverent. And to experience it in *this* Alpha, in whom she'd only witnessed brisk efficiency and brutal decisiveness, turned her world upside-down.

The sticky sound of him removing his pants came from outside the tent, followed by a sodden plop on the ground.

And then he was there, larger and somehow more than he'd been a few moments ago. Laying his hard body flush with hers, he was more, his scent stronger, his heat hotter, his need unfathomable. And not just the massive erection digging into her belly; desire bloomed from his every pore and seasoned the air with every exhale. Kess' Omega sang with recognition, fear a distant memory as slick pooled between her legs.

Capturing her wrists with slow, unhurried movements, he raised them above her head and secured them with one strong hand. With his other, he grasped her chin.

"Why did you leave the fire tonight?" he repeated his question from earlier, his eyes black and dangerous.

"I…" Kess swallowed. "I was thirsty."

A low, threatening growl fanned across her face, but his words were quiet and even. "And there was no other way for you to get water?" he questioned with deadly seriousness. "None at all?"

Dread caved in her chest. Despite his earlier kindness, he was displeased with her, and her Omega quaked inside. She had no real defense of her actions. It had been disobedient and foolhardy, and they both knew it. But what he would do remained a mystery. Her lack of knowledge of him made his actions impossible to predict.

His grip on her wrists tightened, an unspoken signal the question was not rhetorical.

"I wanted to get away from you. I… I was mad… because of the blackberries." The words fell out of her mouth, sounding even stupider than she knew they would.

The harsh lines of his expression, barely discernable in the darkness, transformed into something more animal than man. More rage than reason. More instinct than intelligence. As if all his earlier attentions had been a cover for this angry animal. Foreboding tingled down her captured arms, and she struggled under his grip.

She had escaped one trap only to walk into another. And this one she'd entered voluntarily.

"I was the one protecting you," he seethed, articulating each word as if remaining calm pained him. "Do you know what could've happened tonight, Omega?"

Voice rising at the end, his restraint shattered like a wave against a shore.

Kess mustered all of her remaining bravado. It wasn't much. "I know," she said with as much defiance as she could.

"You *don't* know," he hissed. "He could've fucked you and mated you. Do you understand that? Marked you with his bite. *You would be his, and I wouldn't have been able to do anything about it!*"

Hot breath blasted against her face, each word pummeling her with the truth she knew—she knew better than he did—but didn't want to admit. That's what the attacker had meant when he said he was going to do what Hunter hadn't. He didn't mean only rape her; he meant claim her.

"I understand!" Kess' voice rang out, a surprise to herself. "You think I don't know? You think I don't know what it's like to be minding my own business, swimming in a lake with my friends, only to have an Alpha snatch me away and mount me, sink his filthy teeth into me before I even saw his face?"

She was screaming now, burning tears leaking from her eyes. But his hold on her never relaxed, never faltered. If anything, he grew even larger, his voice clearer and more agonized.

"Then why would you risk it again? Why, Kess?"

Sobs gripped her throat tighter than his hands, and she swallowed to clear them in vain. To clear the guilt and shame and self-recrimination and misery heaving her insides. Years of wretched, horrid, helpless feelings, all sourced from the first minute an Alpha had growled Omega in her ear and her body had responded with a torrent of humiliating slick.

"Because I thought I was safe with you!" The words blistered her throat. Tears ran over her cheeks and soaked her ears as she sputtered and drowned in her own misery.

His chest surged on top of hers as he sucked in large, noisy breaths for several long minutes as if waiting for her tears to stop, for the sobs to crawl back into the quarantined pit of her chest.

Bending, he rested his forehead against hers. When he spoke, his voice was tight, thick, and lethal. "You are safe. From here on out, I swear no harm will come to you, Kess. I'll kill ten more Alphas. A hundred. I don't fucking care. I'll do whatever's necessary to keep you safe." He paused, his grip on her chin shifting to a careful cupping of her cheek. "Including this."

His mouth, growling murder threats a moment before, landed hot and heavy on her own. It wasn't a kiss as much as a claiming. A seal of the promise he'd made. Emotions still raw and quivering, she squeaked at the contact, but her protest got swallowed up, drunk down, consumed, and digested by the massive, heaving Alpha.

Demanding lips sucked the breath from her lungs and robbed her of any further words. Not that she had any anyway. She was too busy swimming in the rich taste of him as his tongue stole into her mouth. He tasted like every beautiful thing—every branching tree and every snowy mountain peak, every surf-encrusted wave, every welcoming fire.

Fire. He tasted like fire, igniting her senses and incinerating them. Arousal licked down her spine, and slick drenched her thighs and the blankets. His lips, his claiming, domineering lips, never stopped moving, never stopped demanding, pressing deeper, tongue tangling with hers as he groaned and flexed his rock-hard cock into her belly.

Panting against her mouth, Hunt wedged his hips between her legs and lined up at her entrance. "I'm gonna fuck you now, Omega. And it's going to be long, and it's going to be hard. And you're going to remember who you belong to."

With one brutal thrust, he breached her channel, and a cry leapt from her throat at the invasion—an invasion she'd dreaded and yearned for in equal measure. He drove forward again, stretching her tight body to seat himself fully inside.

"And you're going to take it like a good Omega who won't ever again... put... herself... in danger." These last four words, he punctuated with harsh thrusts right against her womb.

"Oh, Hunt..." she hissed through pursed lips, on the edge of pleasure and pain.

"That's right," he snarled, digging his face in her neck and tonguing the tender flesh there. "Say my name."

Her hands, still trapped above her head, wiggled and wrested, uselessly trying to escape. Only she didn't want to escape. She wanted to touch his skin and pull his hair and feel his hips pistoning between her palms. Her skin flared, all of it aching and begging for his attention. She flexed her chest, arched her breasts against his grainy chest hair, seeking any kind of stimulation or relief. A heavy palm found one breast and massaged it roughly.

"Is this what you want?" He slapped her breast, pinching her nipple harder and harder until biting pain shot a yelp from her lips. One ounce of pain, and then warmth rolled through her, escalating her buzzing sex into a frenzy. He repeated the torture on the other side, his hips grinding and pounding without pause. Her pelvis rocked under his weight, chasing and bracing against the attack as a climax wound itself into existence.

"News flash, Omega..." One enormous hand anchoring her hips, he paused his thrust, his cockhead resting just inside her entrance. "This isn't for you. This is for me. *Everything* you have is for me. All of it. For me."

She whined, her pelvis straining upward to take more of him, to re-seat his massive member and spurt slick all over his already soaking shaft.

"Yes," he said in her ear, nibbling on the delicate arch. "Say it so I know you understand."

Kess groaned, her body fighting for a release cruelly denied. Fastened between two unforgiving, unyielding Alpha paws, teased by a thick cockhead dangling before her like an overripe fruit on a vine, she whined and squealed and grunted.

"It's yours," she panted. "Please..."

"What's mine?" He nudged her entrance, taunting her with his inhuman restraint. How was he holding back like this? Didn't he want to come? Didn't he want to knot?

Oh God, his knot. The idea of it swelled in her mind, and she keened a plea, almost climaxing right there. She'd never wanted something so much in her entire life.

"What's mine, Omega?"

"I'm yours, Hunter. Everything's yours."

"Fuck yes, it is," he roared with approval and drove forward, the force of his thrusts inching her backward and bunching the blankets under her back.

His grunts escalated, each punch of his hips pushing matching noises out of her throat. She went weightless, the lightning-hot vortex between her thighs shooting everything in all directions. Pleasure, pain, passion, panic—all of it at once and in every fiber of her being. A scream announced her climax, and he drank that up too, his lips again sealed to hers. Sounds poured from her mouth, and she heard them muffled against his as if they came from someone else.

His body snapped into the cradle of her hips, and then, with moans and tremors and gulping breaths, he was coming too. The beginnings of the knot inflated inside of her, bringing that impossible, stretching, incredible fullness. It ground against her internal nerves and extended her climax on and on and on beneath the imprisoning knot that locked them together.

Hunt froze above her, his face contorted in agonized ecstasy, enough that his hands loosened and she pried herself away. Her fingers dove for his hair, seeking the soft texture of his thick, silvery locks and clenching them in her sweaty, greedy fists. Foreheads resting together, they breathed each other's breath as his hips trembled with spurt after hot spurt.

Circling, pulsing gently, he rocked against her, seating the knot deeper as it expanded, and she crumbled against him again with renewed shudders and soft, pleading whines.

"Oh God," she whimpered, knees falling farther apart, her pelvis open and filled. "It's too much. I can't—"

"Shhh…" He swiped his tongue over her open lips. "You can. Such a good Omega. Just a little more now…"

Full to bursting, her body laid to waste, limp and drained from climax after climax, her muscles went loose. Only her fingertips buried in Hunt's hair held on like they alone tethered her to reality.

It had never been like this before. Tears dripped from her eyes as the realization crashed over her. Brock had fucked her, knotted her hundreds and hundreds of times. Same as Hunter, whispering dirty words and demands in her ears, and she'd orgasmed for him too.

Yet something was different.

When Hunter had asked, she'd told him, *I'm yours*, same as she'd told Brock. But this time… she'd believed it. Not until those words escaped had she even known that all the other interactions with Brock, the same sentiments exchanged, had been a pale pantomime compared to whatever this was. She'd been Brock's like she'd been his horse or his favorite knife. A possession to use and care for and show off.

But Hunter… she was his like his own blood. Circulating inside him, a living thing that bathed his tissues and kept him alive. A living thing that could not be separated from him, lest it end both of their lives.

"You're mine now," he whispered in her ear, shudders still racking his body.

She dragged a heel up the back of his leg and back down again, unable to deny it. "I am."

"Good." A single, guttural syllable before the sharp bite of his teeth sunk into her flesh. Jawbones bore down, and her flesh gave way. Skin and muscle and blood vessels popped and separated under the force of the controlled attack. Kess cried out, the pain melding into the bliss still running rampant up and down her spine and filling her with deep, rending satisfaction.

That satisfaction bound her to him until one of them died. The idea drove into her like an icicle to the eye. Given her good fortune being widowed from one horrid Alpha, she doubted she'd be so lucky a second time. Her Omega shrieked, appalled at the very idea of wishing death on her Alpha.

But Kess couldn't stop it. She'd believed it when she'd told Hunt she was his. And the truth made it all the viler.

CHAPTER 16

Hunter

The morning was clear and still as the Pack left the campsite. It was as if, after witnessing his brutality the day prior, the forest sought to lurk below his awareness. The Pack too went about their duties, efficient and subdued. No one spoke of Van or what had been done to dispose of the body. Hunt, quite frankly, didn't give a solitary fuck. They could leave the carcass out for the wolves as far as he was concerned. Van's things were collected and the horses loaded up, the new pup Heck inheriting the dead Alpha's mount. Which seemed fitting, given the pup's role in disrupting the assault and watching over his Omega as she panicked and ran.

As Kess' clothes were still damp and reeking of male violence, Hunt dressed her in a spare shirt of his own. It hung on her dainty frame and fell off her shoulders. He conspicuously pulled the collar to the side to expose the oozing bite mark and display it for the Pack's notice.

And notice they did. He watched their eyes alight on the mark and slide away, some with grim confirmation of what they'd already anticipated, some with barely concealed surprise, some with shock at the savagery.

He understood. Whatever human part remained inside him recoiled at the barbarism, yet he couldn't keep his own eyes off of it. It equal parts thrilled and disturbed him.

Occasionally he tended to the wound, kissing and lapping in an attempt to staunch the trickling blood and soothe the torn and reddened flesh. Each drop of Kess' blood coated his tongue and reminded him of the heated spurt that had shot in his mouth the night before. When his lips detached from the vicious wound with a final, gentle sweep, a bone-deep growl quaked through his chest, and one word echoed in his head: Mine.

She's mine.

The knowledge sang inside him, filling him with a sensation of such pure, unmitigated rightness, he wanted to cry. Where had this Omega come from? And what had he ever done in his life to deserve her?

Like the rest of the Pack, Kess' silence spoke volumes. She'd permitted another round of mating this morning, when it became clear to Hunt that going without would not be a viable option, his dick so hard he wondered if it would infarct itself. In the blue-gray morning, she'd submitted to him, soft and languid in his arms, her back against his front, sighing and mewling as her cunt milked his knot for all it was worth. Nose buried in her neck, with the taste of her scent and her blood on his lips, he'd honestly thought his brains might liquify right out of his nose.

She flinched away as he pressed another kiss to her shoulder, and resignation shoved hard between his shoulder blades. Despite her impassioned words last night, she hadn't wanted this. Drunk on ecstasy, she'd declared she was his, but she hadn't wanted to belong to an Alpha ever again. He understood that intellectually. Yet the events of the night had unhinged his intellect from his instinct, and it was too late to turn back.

Nonetheless, her silence stung. What had he expected from her, though? Gratitude? Relief? Elation?

He inched forward, pressing up against her back and wrapping an arm around her belly. "It hurts?"

She responded with a nod, her soft hair brushing against his face.

"I'm sorry for that," he said, and meant it. The idea of her pain disturbed him more than murdering a member of his own Pack. "You wear my mark now. No Alpha will touch you, in this Pack or any other. Meant what I said, Kess. You're safe now."

"I know." Her voice was little more than a soft sigh.

"You're sad." A statement, not a question. Her uninjured shoulder lifted in the briefest of shrugs. "I know you didn't want this."

At this, she sagged. Hunt twisted the reins gathered in his free hand. Would his every attempt at a consoling word only make her collapse further in on herself? He wished she would just talk to him.

"Alpha." Colt rode up alongside him, cutting a quick glance at the sullen Omega and back to Hunt. "The new pup says there's a pretty sizeable village about a day's ride north of here. Wondering what you think about turning up that way."

Hunt grunted. "What's that pup know about sizeable?"

"Says he's been there a few times for trade. There ain't much out this way otherwise, got no reason to doubt him."

Hunt squeezed the Omega's thigh. "You know this place, Kess?"

"I know people in the village would go there a few times a year, yes." She swallowed around a catch in her voice. "Never went myself, so I can't speak to its size."

Pleased to hear her voice again, he hummed a low purr of approval, absently stroking his palm up and down her thigh. Without saying as much, the Omega didn't like the idea. He couldn't speculate as to why, but apprehension sizzled off her like heat off a high-beam lamp.

He didn't particularly feel like heading into another Beta village himself, all things considered. Settlements provided trade, but also liquor and women—and, God forbid, more Omegas and more drama. Hunt had already had his fill of all of that for the trip.

He turned back to Colt. "You like the idea."

"I like the idea of replacing that spoilt grain sooner rather than later."

"Fair enough," Hunt relented. About the only thing that interested him this moment was a few nights alone with his Omega and no other distractions.

Which was a damned good idea.

"You all go on ahead," Hunt proposed. "Take the Pack north, check out this settlement, then head on. I'm gonna take Kess and keep heading west toward the ocean. We can meet up outside of Old Tacoma in a week for the rest of the way home. How's that sound?"

Colt's eyes narrowed, and he flicked another glance at Kess. Hunt's temper flared, and he cleared his throat loudly. Motherfucker needed to keep his eyes and mind off his Omega.

Colt didn't so much as lift an eyebrow, returning an impassive gaze.

Hunt tilted his head at the line of Alphas behind them. "Think you can handle these mongrels?"

A smile played at the corner of Colt's lips. "Got no worries on that account. Anything you want me to pick up for you in the settlement?"

"The Omega needs new clothes. And shoes. And a coat if you can scare one up. Everything she has are almost rags."

Kess bristled, but she stayed silent. She could hardly argue otherwise.

"Here." Hunt unsnapped a saddlebag and pulled out a leather sheath, handing it to Colt. "There's three good knives in there to trade. And any of those baskets we loaded up back at the pup's village, feel free to trade those as well."

Roused from silence, Kess turned to catch his eye. "My baskets?"

"Yeah, Alek fetched them from your place." He drew his hand up and notched it in her waist. "Unless you need them for some other reason?"

She gave a cute little head shake, her curls bouncing, her expression inscrutable.

"Let me load you up some food and tell the others." Colt guided his horse away.

Kess faced forward again. "I can't believe you went back for my baskets."

"They're beautiful. Would be a waste to leave them in that hellhole, especially since you put so much work into them."

Hunt couldn't see from his vantage, but he swore he felt her smile. His suspicion was confirmed when her weight sank back against his chest slightly. Unreasonably pleased by such a small thing, Hunt circled his hand around her waist to cup the small swell of her belly. Too small, in his opinion. He really did need to feed her more. Omegas were not naturally predisposed to scrawniness, and he knew the mouthwatering places her body naturally wanted to plump and round.

They slid back into silence, there not being much else to say on the topic of her baskets. Colt delivered a pack bulging with food, giving him a friendly nod goodbye. After securing the provisions, Hunt kicked Cleo into a trot, happy to steal his Omega away from the Pack without a backward glance.

Kess seized the pommel as Cleo picked up the pace, her hands abnormally sluggish in responding. It wasn't only her grip that suffered. She felt weak everywhere. Exhausted. Depleted. Drained. The weariness so bone-deep she failed to parse its exact origin—mental or physical, or both.

In the space of twelve hours, she'd survived an almost-rape, fled through an unknown forest, been proximal to her assailant's murder, and been unambiguously claimed with a vicious bite. An extraordinary amount to assimilate, even if it hadn't come on the heels of being outed as an Omega and uprooted from her quiet, solitary life in the Beta village. And now Hunter had decided to depart from the Pack and divert them on an alternate route to the coast. Contemplating his motivations required too much energy, let alone protesting the change in plans. If she even cared. She wasn't much sure she did. After the assault by the creek, she'd just as well avoid Packs.

Then again, no other Alpha, in Hunt's Pack or otherwise, would dare lay hands on her now. As if to agree, her fresh bite mark throbbed at the thought. She couldn't sense it herself, but Brock explained an Omega's scent changed when she bore an Alpha's mark, emitting an aversive "keep away" signal to other Alphas. Brock complained her signal had been weak, or at least weaker than he would've liked. Knowing little about Alpha-Omega bonds, she couldn't explain it one way or another. But to him, it symbolized another deficiency of hers.

Hunter divulged no such dissatisfaction. In fact, he seemed unable to keep his attention off her bite mark, nuzzling and licking it every few minutes. If anything, he radiated a prideful satisfaction with it, making sure to adjust her clothing so it would be visible to his Pack. Given the smug slant to his firm lips, she sensed this behavior broadcast as much bravado as deterrent. Even stranger, she had the sense he wasn't only proud of the marking, but he was proud of her. He'd said as much when talking about her baskets. Appreciating her handiwork, he'd sent Alek back to retrieve them without her even asking and, recognizing their value, offered them in trade. They're beautiful, he'd said, and warmth had bloomed in her cheeks, flattered he saw the time and attention she'd devoted to their construction.

Maybe he wasn't so bad after all.

The sudden rush of fondness caught her up short. This was Hunter she was talking about. A brutal, possessive, violent, murdering Alpha. What was she doing, acquiescing to this coarse beast on the basis of a kind word and a few orgasms? What was happening to her? Even now, atop the horse, she rested against him and savored his delicious scent when she ought to be plotting her escape.

Yet every time his skin touched hers, she lost herself, each time more than the last. Lost in her Omega nature, she submitted. Thoroughly. Joyfully. Again and again. Echoes of her own words haunted her. Begging him to take her, to take what was "his." I'm yours, Hunter, she'd said, her body open and ready. She needed no further proof of that than the sweet, gentle kiss Hunter placed on the bite, his lips sparking a riotous trembling that worked its way from her head to her toes. The bite she'd asked for, begged for.

In the light of day, she couldn't hide from what she'd done. Despite her promise to never belong to an Alpha again, she'd yielded. Offered herself up for the taking and bore the mark as a result. She'd placed herself in his hands without even asking what that meant. Would he restrict her freedom, confine her as Brock had done? Mate her through cycle after cycle to try for pups? Did he even want pups? And if not, then what did he want with her?

Cleo jostled over the terrain, and a wave of queasiness rose from her stomach. She wiped a bead of sweat from her hairline, swallowing down bile burning the back of her throat. Rising nausea spurred by the increasingly hysterical path of her thoughts. Another sign of how taxed she was, body and soul.

The smarting, burning bite mark pulsed again and reinforced the awful, sick feeling. Was she going to throw up right on top of the horse? Was the bite making her ill? Was it her roiling emotions? Or was it the new and different—and plentiful—food? Hunter wasted no opportunity to shove snacks in her mouth. She'd barely finished breakfast when he was handing her a pouch of more nuts and jerky, grumbling something about bony Omegas being unnatural. Too tired to fight, she'd dutifully eaten whatever he had given her, enjoying the foreign sensation of over-fullness.

At least, she had been enjoying it. Now her stomach heaved in protest. Fading out of consciousness, she slumped against Hunter's solid chest. She'd devise a plan when she felt better. Maybe after a nap.

*

They rode the rest of the morning and afternoon. With each clop of Cleo's hooves, Kess sank further and further into him. He'd absorbed her pleasing weight, letting himself bask in the enjoyment of this small evidence of trust and comfort.

Eventually she grew languid enough to loll her head against his shoulder. He'd studied her face, noting the pinked-up blotches on her cheeks and the perspiration kissing her hairline, and concern brewed in his belly. When questioned, she'd brushed off his worries, muttering about the sun or lack of sleep. Which he couldn't argue with. She wasn't used to exhausting days in the saddle, but still… some unnamed worry niggled him.

Rife with unease, he aborted the day's travels several hours before dusk. They'd made good progress, moving faster without the entire Pack at their tail, and he estimated they were about one more day's ride from the coast. He hoped the fresh salt air would perk up his drooping wildflower, but the argument rang false even in his own head.

Hunt eased the sluggish Omega off the horse and laid her out on the hastily unrolled bedding.

"Kess, baby," he crooned, wiping her damp forehead. "You don't look well. Do you hurt anywhere?"

Eyes closed, she moaned gently, her lips parted and starting to crack. "Just tired… and hot. So hot."

He pressed a hand to her cheek, and she was indeed burning up. Anxiety scalded him from the inside. Fever equaled infection. But infected with what? Where? Frantic, he dug under her clothes, searching her skin for any blemish or sign of purulence and finding none. None except the angry bite mark he himself had made. Such a source of pride for him, now he glared at the mark, furious with himself.

Fetching fresh water, he cleaned the wound, dabbing gently around the newly formed scabs. No fluctuant pocket hid under the flesh, and no pus exuded when he prodded it deeper, although he did manage to elicit an agonized cry from his Omega with his poking around. Reddened and swollen and scabbing, sure, but not obviously infected. He cursed himself for lapping it with his dirty, filthy mouth throughout the day. He ought've known better, if he'd bothered to remember any of his medical training. One didn't clean a wound with human saliva!

Although he wasn't quite human anymore, was he? And, he couldn't explain it, but instinct urged him to tend to her shoulder in this way. Something deep in his brain scratching to make sure he kept the healing flesh moistened. Even as he stood over her, sick with worry, his lips longed to kiss and soothe the angry skin with his tongue.

A low groan escaped from Kess' lips and climbed into a full wail. She rolled on her side, curling up and clutching at her belly.

"Nooooo…"

"Kess," he pleaded, "what is it? What hurts?" Heart galloping in his chest, Hunt hunched over her, terrified by uselessness.

"Cramps," she bit out through gritted teeth. "Feels like cramps."

Cramps? Like menstrual cramps? Cramping could mean anything from food poisoning to appendicitis to a bowel obstruction. So many things to harm his Omega out here in the wilderness. Shit. Maybe they shouldn't have left the Pack. He glanced at the tree line from which they'd come. How long would it take to ride back to rejoin the Pack? What would that even do? No one in the Pack would be any use whatsoever.

What if…?

The sentence refused to complete itself. His fears were so numerous, he couldn't even name one. He was panicking, plain and simple.

"Okay, baby." Hunt rubbed her thigh. "What can I do? What helps?"

"Don't... know..."

Hunt's eyes scanned the campsite he'd chosen, searching for anything, anything that all that would help his suffering Omega. Propelled by near-hysteric impotence, he left her side to gather firewood. It would be dark soon, and they'd need a fire. He paced the area, grabbing wood and racing back to Kess' side with every pained cry, no better able to help than he was the first time.

Cramps, it's just cramps, he silently chanted over and over like a pathetic prayer. He wished, for the first time in a long time, for something as basic as Tylenol or ibuprofen. Or even a heating pad. He'd had a college girlfriend who'd wrap herself around a heating pad every month. Spying some large, flat rocks under a tree, he grabbed one and dusted it off before pushing it into the fire. Maybe he could improvise a heat source for Kess.

Between bites of dried meat and fruit to settle his own stomach, Hunt dribbled water into Kess' mouth and draped her forehead with a cool cloth. Occasionally her glassy eyes opened to stare at him in gratitude, and anxiety slit him open all over again. He couldn't lose her already.

Cramps, it's just cramps.

When the rock heated, he wrapped it in a blanket, burning his fingertips in the process, and laid it under her shirt against her abdomen. She hissed as the warmth touched her skin, but—realizing the potential relief—adjusted the stone's position and clutched it tighter to her pelvis. After several minutes, the pain lines in her forehead eased, and she drifted into a heavy sleep. Hunt released a long breath, enjoying the smallest bit of relief.

After tidying the camp, he lay down beside her, forgoing the tent. Kess curled over the warmed stone, Hunter curled over Kess. Inhale after inhale of her sweet, heady scent lulled him, and he savored this small taste of peace. He held it in his mouth, unwilling to swallow and relinquish the barest of signs that his Omega would pull through.

CHAPTER 17

Kess

Her body woke before she did. Not her entire body, necessarily, but her sex for sure. Swimming through a cloudy, dreamlike haze, her naked body throbbed with winding tension working its way through every cell. Kess hovered in a state between wakefulness and sleep, reaching out to the Alpha responsible for all the glorious desire pounding underneath her skin.

She wanted him. Every hair on his body, every inch of his skin, every expression on his face. She wanted to glut herself on all of it. Grab large handfuls and rub herself all over him. Just the idea buzzed between her legs and sent shimmers of a small, inadequate climax in its wake.

Sex aglow and twitching with the paltry release, Kess walked back through the door of reality. Her eyes popped open, looking into the shining blue of her Alpha's, bright in the early morning gray. Building tension began anew between her legs, driven by her own hips making small, lewd pulses against the manly thigh she'd straddled in her sleep. A massive hand gripped her hip, not to stop her movements, but seemingly to go along for the ride, or even coax her rocking into something harsher, deeper, lewder.

"Kess," he whispered, his throat scratched and abraded. "Are you feeling better?"

Kess pulled at her clothes and their suffocating constraints. Every touch, every fiber against her skin that wasn't Hunter's body was a sin, a travesty, a fucking *outrage*.

"Get these off," she demanded, frustrated as her thick, clumsy fingers fumbled the buttons. All the while her hips ground against the thick muscles bulging between her legs, a more satisfying release just out of reach.

Blue eyes flaring with white-hot flame, Hunt whipped the shirt off her body and unlaced the ties of her pants. Moving to pull them all the way off, she wailed at the removal of his thigh, torn between wanting the garment gone and wanting to keep him seated exactly where he was. Cool air glided over her skin, highlighting the heat coursing through her. Heat.

She was in Heat. Incomprehensible yet undeniable, her Heat responses were unchanged even after years without. She'd think about it later, how and why her Heat had returned. For now, she wanted only one thing, and he watched her with the same want reflected in his gaze.

"Are you sure you're okay?" Chest filling with great gulps of air, Hunter's greedy eyes swept over her exposed body, lingering on areas of interest. He peeled out of his clothes, still not touching her. Tempting him to action, Kess palmed handfuls of her breasts and shoved them higher on her chest, pointing her inpatient nipples in his direction in overt enticement.

"Not okay," she panted, whipping her head back and forth. Her thumbs played with the hardened points, pinching and pulling in a weak approximation of what she wanted. "Suck these. *Now*. Please."

With a guttural noise, Hunt dove for her, his hunger matching her own. Batting her hands away, he commandeered the sensitive mounds and pressed them together, sucking a nipple fast and hard. Kess wailed at the deep, inexcusable pleasure. He sucked and pulled, first one, then the other, back and forth again and again. Kess arched and thrashed under him. So good and still not enough.

Snaking her hands between them, her fingertips sought her own private inferno, drenched in slick and more pouring forth with every hot pull of his tongue. She attacked her own flesh with an alarming aggressiveness, circling and rubbing the swollen flesh with one hand and delving inside with the other.

"What the fuck are you doing?" Hunt growled, eyes opening from his nipple-sucking trance to see her frenzied hands hard at work. He snarled again, those delicious thighs kicking hers apart. Cool air blasted over her burning-up body, both a welcome relief and another incomprehensible sensation to absorb.

"I need..." She couldn't describe her own need. Couldn't make the words of what she needed. Because she didn't need.

She *was* need.

"You're in Heat, Omega." Hunt settled between her legs, the hot length of him immediately nudging her entrance.

"I know." Crazy for him, crazy for his cock, Kess thrust and bucked up into the thick slab of Hunt's abdomen and pelvis. "Stop talking and fuck me."

He exhaled in frustration, sounding like a chuffing horse. "Jesus, woman, *hold still.*"

A whine peeled from her throat as he clamped a hand on her hip, stilling her long enough to sheath himself in one easy, slick-drenched glide. They moaned together at the tight fit.

"Oh my God, Hunter." Kess wiggled against the invasion, full to bursting. Overfull. Positively stuffed. How could he feel even bigger than last night? That wasn't possible... was it? He slid out and in, one smooth thrust, laying waste to the last vestiges of her reason. "You feel so good."

"*Fuck me*, baby." He reared upright on his knees, hooking her behind the thighs with his powerful hands and spreading her legs out and even wider. The stretch in her groin added to the stretch in her channel, and all of it blurred into one endless, mindless rush. With sharp thrusts and yanks, he both rocked into her and tugged her deeper onto him, sealing their bodies as close together as possible with every stab. With a flex of his veiny forearms, he manipulated her body as if she weighed nothing.

Poised above her, the vast spread of his chest and the bulges of his abdominals mesmerized her. She'd yet to see him like this in daylight, in his full glory, all that Alpha strength and muscle on proud display. Her eyes drank him in, torn between focusing on his striving body working her over or on the place of their joining, where his impossibly hard dick slammed in and out and filled her to the brim. Distracted, she caught flashes of his dusky sack as it rocked under the violent motion, slapping against her bottom, heavy and taut with impending discharge.

Her eyes dragged upwards and met his. Blue-gray and deadly, they burned like dying embers in a hazy, foggy dawn.

His lip curled up in a snarl. "That feel good, Omega? This what you want? Take my knot and come all over my cock? That's what you want, baby?"

Her fingers clawed to touch him but spread out like a pinned butterfly; there wasn't much she could reach. Her nails found the ridges of his abdomen, and she scraped a vicious path down his corrugated muscles. Gratified she could at least do this. Could make some mark on him. A trickle of blood beaded on him, mixing with his sweat and her slick and tinging the area pink.

It was heinous. Depraved. Violent and brutal.

And she loved every second.

Climax birthed itself from deep in her womb, rumbling like distant thunder before the storm. Entire sex on fire, her hips bounced up to meet his with what little movement she could manage and pushed her right over the edge. The ice blue of his eyes held hers through the convulsions as she wailed and thrashed against him. His expression, wild and severe, monitored every twitch of her face and the body under his control.

"Good, Omega." He slowed his thrusts and withdrew, tearing a pathetic mewl from her lips at his absence. Without waiting for her to come down, he flipped her over to her knees and elbows, maneuvering her body ass-up in submission. With a groan that betrayed his fracturing control, he reentered her body and began to pound. The angle hit different. More intimate. Deeper. She pitched back against him in time with his thrusts, trying to take him deeper still. "I like you like this, baby. I like seeing everything that's mine."

Already moistened with the slick coating her from navel to the small of her back, a finger passed over her tight back hole. She yelped in surprise at the unexpected and confusing sensation.

"This is mine too, baby," he said softly, with a quiet menace, his thumb circling and circling. Her brain fizzed to accommodate the experience of a thing she ought not to like, but... did. "Does that feel good? I think you like it. How about this...?"

A few more circles and he nudged inside, barely anything, but she felt the breach like she'd been waiting her whole life for it. If her head hadn't already been scrambled, she would've passed out. Slowly he pushed farther in, pumping the finger in time with his brutal hips, each dip delving further and further. Knuckle after knuckle of sweet, welcome invasion.

"Hungry Omega," he growled. "Hungry cunt and hungry ass. Ready to gobble up everything I've got."

As if she hadn't already come mere minutes ago, his words brought her close to the brink. She wiggled and snorted to impale herself further on his body. Mad, crazy, insane ideas jammed themselves in her head. She wished he had two cocks so she could take a knot from each one at the same time. Captured and speared like a prize hunt. And another one for her mouth, so she could suck and nurse and drink him down at the same time as he filled her up. Her lips ached to taste him again, to remember the feel of his slippery come on her tongue as it spurted down her throat and warmed her belly.

"Come here," he ordered, pausing to pull her up until he could reach an arm around her torso. Though Kess was unsteady and hanging off his cock, his arm anchored her balance enough for her not to fall on her face. As if he could read her mind, his other hand breached her lips. Unable to move on her own, secured between his hands and cock, she was a creature totally under his control and on the brisk of dissolving totally.

"This is mine too, yeah? You're in Heat, baby. Your Omega Heat is here, and I'm going to fuck you through it until you lose your voice from screaming my name."

In response, Kess sucked, tasting the salt of his body and the feel of his flesh between her teeth. She wanted to bite, to mark and destroy, but not here. Not his hand. She needed different flesh for that. So she sucked and licked and slid her lips over his digits like it was another cock, eliciting such sounds from Hunt, he seemed a creature not human but of the forest. An animal. A true Alpha predator laying waste to anything in his path.

And she'd run directly into his trap.

"Such a good little Omega," he panted. "Are you ready for me? Are you ready for my knot in your tight little pussy?"

Kess moaned an affirmative around his fingers before he removed them and she fell forward. Back on her elbows, face buried in the blankets, he rode her into the ground. A growling hunger sucked at her insides. She would take anything he gave her. And then more. She'd lay herself open, and he could take and take and take.

"I'm ready," she cried. "Don't stop! Please!"

Light exploded behind her eyelids, and the world disappeared. Kess ceased to exist for long moments of curling, shattering pleasure. Grunting, crying, shouting, and screaming, she came and came, tensing around the thick member that was the source of her entire existence.

"So... fucking... tight," Hunt ground out, his body quaking and shuddering with powerful, controlled, masculine violence. His knot bulged at her entrance, and he tipped his hips to shove it deeper into her canal, setting off another flurry of pulses in her sex. Completely unhinged, she ground backward against him, desperate for him to bury every last inch inside her as they panted and cooled from their respective releases.

After a moment, knot fully seated, Hunt eased her down to her stomach and plastered himself to her back. His breath tickled her neck and cooled the sweat under her hair when he gathered it to the side.

All she could smell was Hunt. In her nose, on her skin, under her fingernails, in her pussy. His woodsy musk, even more potent in the aftermath, was everywhere, and she couldn't get enough.

"I never thought..." he purred in her ear, voice rumbling from his chest into hers. "I never thought it could really be like this."

"A Heat?"

"Sex," he corrected, "with a *mate*."

The word *mate* pinged uncomfortable memories of another Alpha snarling it in her ear, along with his demands and disappointments. She'd always hated the knotting process with Brock, being tied to him while it took its time to deflate. Other Omegas would be starry-eyed talking about it, a time when they would talk to their Alpha and bask in their focused attention.

"It's not always like this," she whispered, resting her head on folded arms.

Hunter was silent for a long moment, his lips never stilling as he kissed along her neck, across her shoulder, and up into her hairline.

"Someday," he said thoughtfully, his deep voice wrapping around her like a blanket, "I hope you will tell me what happened with your last Pack. I know I can't do anything to undo it, but... I would like to know, and it might help you to tell me. When you're ready."

"I'll never be ready," she shot back, the words out of her mouth before she had a chance to truly consider his, quite frankly, kind and sensitive offer.

"Okay, baby," he said, continuing his caresses as if she hadn't said anything remotely rude or dismissive. A resonant purr started within his chest and reverberated into her taxed body. It rumbled over her like a massage, and she couldn't resist its allure. "Get some rest, sweetheart. You're gonna need it."

CHAPTER 18

Hunter

Hunt purred Kess into listless sleep while his knot receded, unsure of what else to do. His Packmates had hosted Omegas before, so he was vaguely familiar with the way a Heat proceeded, but he'd never been so close to the actual flame. At least, close to the flame of an Omega who wasn't so lust-crazed as to endanger her own life.

In typical circumstances, the Alpha-Omega pair would lock themselves away in their cabin, only to emerge a week later looking a bit worse for the wear, but otherwise smug and self-satisfied. But the question of what actually ensued during the week of seclusion, he had no answer to. Other than the nonstop fucking, of course.

Knot deflated, he detached from the softly snoring Omega with as much delicacy as he could manage. Wiping chilled sweat from his own neck and back, he took stock of the campsite. It wasn't ideal—he would've preferred something with a roof and bed—but it would have to do. Depending on how crazed she woke up, maybe they could travel a few more hours westward and find somewhere with more natural shelter.

A pitiful moan broke through her lips, the naked Omega's pelvis obscenely flexing against the ground, even in her sleep.

Probably no on the travel, then.

Filled with urgency, Hunt quickly staked the tent and tended to the munching Cleo. If the skies broke open with rain, he'd at least like to be able to keep the Omega dry. After yesterday's panic about possible infection, he needed to ensure she would be healthy for the duration of the Heat. And God help him if he entered a Rut along with her, as he had no idea who would ensure either of them ate or drank.

At least her fever had broken. But had it truly been a fever, or a sign that heralded her impending Heat? The severe cramping made a certain amount of sense in retrospect, even if it still slayed him to helplessly witness Kess' discomfort.

After checking again on the stirring Omega, he retrieved some pegs and string from his bag and stalked into the surrounding woods. Colt had packed them enough nonperishable food, but he'd need to get something fresh and nutritive into her. The snares would be his best bet to pick off some unsuspecting rabbits. Hopefully they would have a bit of meat on them. If not, he'd try his luck at fishing, although that could take more time than he feared he would have.

"Hunt! Hunter!" A panicked cry rang through the woods, and in one second, Hunt was on his feet, hustling back to Kess.

When he broke through the trees, she made a beeline for him and hurled her naked body against his chest.

"I woke up and you were gone." Her words were muffled, but the accusation stung nonetheless.

"I wasn't gone," he explained, rubbing her goose-fleshed back. "I was setting some snares for food. You have to eat."

"Okay," she breathed, notching her nose at the base of his neck and inhaling deeply. Pleased with her findings, she hummed a low tune and began brushing her hard nipples over his torso. "I'll eat whatever you put in my mouth."

Hunt instantly hardened, hastened by her innuendo and the heady scent of their mating still clinging to her skin. Tipping his head back, he noted big pupils behind heavy-lidded eyes. The Omega was barely awake and already begging for more.

"Kess." His hands circled her arms and angled her away from his chest. "First you eat and drink something, all right?"

Not waiting for agreement, he led her over to the campsite and supervised as she drank down two canteens of water. After some initial pouts and whines, she submitted to his hydration requirements. If nothing else, she'd need to stay hydrated to replenish all the liquid spilling from between her legs. Afterward, he fed her some dried meat, hard cheese, and some mushy blackberries Colt had added to the provisions. Berry juice dribbled down her chin and spilled onto her breasts as she took the food directly from his hand.

He'd discovered the only way to get her to eat and not get distracted was to cradle her between his knees and feed her himself. Completely nude and unconcerned with that fact, her body thrummed with sexual readiness, nipples taut and her sex swollen in expectation. To keep her somewhat sated and agreeable to taking in sustenance, he toyed with the tender points of her breasts and smeared the berry juice over her smooth brown skin.

Lost in the Heat haze, he hardly recognized the woman he'd met cowering in her hut, or the defiant runaway he'd rode behind that first day on the trail, accusing him of feeling entitled to take whatever he wanted simply by happenstance of being an Alpha. Sure, he'd insisted she leave the village with him, but her current disposition made no pretense of not wanting his Alpha attentions.

She let out a frustrated groan and dodged the last blackberry with a sharp head turn. "No more. I'm full."

Hunt popped the berry into his mouth and licked his stained fingers, Kess tracking his every motion with her avid eyes. Hard as a rock the entire time, somehow his dick got even harder at this. He wasn't sure he'd be able to keep off her for much longer. The restless squirming against his crotch wasn't helping the situation.

Hunt drifted a hand down between her legs, stroking the dense curls there in a languid motion to keep her distracted. "How long do your Heats usually last?"

Kess tossed her head side to side. "It's been so long, I don't know. Thought I was too old."

"Like hell." Hunt snorted. "How old are you?"

She paused in her lusty writhing, her brows folding in on themselves for a different reason than sexual agony. "Forty? Somewhere thereabouts, give or take."

Hunt chuckled and rubbed a thumb over her berry-stained lips. "You're in Heat now, baby, whether you like it or not."

Her pretty pink tongue darted out to lick his thumb, sending electricity skittering up his arm. "Why do you call me baby? I'm obviously not a baby. I just told you how old I am."

At this, he laughed so loud, he startled her and probably a few woodland creatures. Pitying her sweet, confused expression, he immediately purred and gathered her closer to offer comfort. "Where I'm from," he explained, "people used to call their lovers *babe* or *baby* as an affectionate nickname. But that was a long time ago." His voice drifted as the lightness dimmed in remembrance of all that had passed since TheEnd. "I guess no one does that anymore. Would you like me to stop?"

He gazed down into her round eyes, the rich brown of her irises surrounding her arousal-wide pupils. In his entire life, he'd never seen a more beautiful female, Beta or Omega or even human before TheEnd. Even considering the carefully coiffed and groomed women he'd dated in his prior life filled him with confusing but potent disgust. Those women had absolutely nothing to compare to his wanton, wild-haired, sweet-smelling Omega.

"I don't mind." Her lips twitched in a small smile. "It's… unique."

"Not as unique as you, baby," he said, hoarse with unexpected emotion. Her face, open and so fucking pretty, glowed in the sunshine. His eyes swept her nakedness as his fingertips breezed across her belly and hips. No question, he was already drunk on her body. Taking in her luscious, perfect curves, his cock urged some sort of forward momentum, but he held back. After eating, Kess was more lucid and less lust-crazed than she had been, as evidenced by her ability to have this conversation without dry-humping the air. This might be his only chance to talk to her for another day.

"You don't remember your last Heat?"

Twisting in his arms, her tongue grazed his nipple. The shocking stimulation made him grit his teeth to stay focused.

"Definitely before Brock died, so at least five years? I thought they were over." Her voice pitched into a lazy, dreamy tone, and she began speaking in between planting sucking kisses and little nibbles on his nipple. "But I haven't been around any Alphas either, so…"

"Hmm…" His hips ground upward in an involuntary, stimulation-seeking flex, his control slipping rapidly. "How long did they last when you had them?"

"Four days, I think. But if he went into a full-on Rut, it might be a few more. I'm not entirely sure, though; they were always hard to remember afterward." Her head dropped back from driving him slowly insane with nipple torture, and she smoothed back some hair that had fallen on his cheek. "Your hair is so pretty," she mused. "I've never seen a gray-haired Alpha. How old are you?"

"Older than you'd imagine." He smiled indulgently. Now wasn't the time to have this conversation.

In fact, he'd reached his limit for conversation. He bent his head and covered her curvy mouth with his own. Her taste tingled on his tongue, ripened with the tart berries and the potency of her Heat pheromones. She responded to his kiss, delving a tongue into his mouth and making him groan.

His fingers slipped between her legs, finding her hot, wet, and sensitive to his touch. She parted her thighs instinctively and hissed her approval when he slipped a finger inside.

"Do you want to ride me this time, baby?" he whispered against her lips.

She gasped in surprise. "You'd let me? Most Alphas—"

"I don't give a fuck about most Alphas," he said, licking the delicate line of her jaw. "I want to watch your tits bounce while you get off. Sound good to you?"

"Yes," she said, grabbing his head between her two palms and attacking his mouth with more hot, wet kisses. "Oh yes."

CHAPTER 19

Kess

Bright morning sunbeams glared directly into her sticky eyes. A full bladder demanded immediate attention while an enormous Alpha snored in her ear. Harsh sensations assaulting her on all sides, Kess relented to consciousness.

Heaving the dead weight of Hunt's arm off her, she scooted out of the tent to relieve herself. Bladder full to bursting, it truly was a relief. Blurry memories surfaced of the Alpha urging her to drink water over and over again, along with memories of many other things they did over and over again.

Kess scratched her itchy scalp, and let out a small shriek as her fingers discovered the clumped and deranged state it had worked itself into. A disheveled gray head popped out between the tent flaps.

"What is it?" His eyes darted to the tree line, apparently looking for intruders. One small yelp, and the formerly snoring Alpha came fully awake and ready to pounce. "Are you all right?"

A strange sensation percolated in her chest as he emerged, quite nude, and stalked around the campsite like the predator he was. A twinge in her shoulder drew her attention to where her hand had unconsciously sought out his mark. She couldn't see it from her vantage, but poking around the area, she was surprised to find it nearly healed. How many days had she been in Heat?

"Did you see something?" Apparently satisfied by his patrol, Hunter approached, his presence becoming more and more massive with every step. Toe to toe, she had to tilt her head back to see his eyes, glued to her and tense with concern.

"No, nothing." If she'd been concerned about her own hair, his might've been in an even worse state. Wiry silver strands sprang out in all directions. Combined with the overgrown beard, it lent him a savage, grizzled caveman look. A smile pulled at her lips, and she poked to her own head, "My hair is in quite a state."

His brows tucked together, and his head tilted as if he couldn't understand what she'd said. But after a pointed perusal of her curls, his consternation lifted with a wry tilt to his lips.

"If you're worrying about your hair, then I expect your Heat is finished."

Reference to her Heat and the past days of debauchery sent blood to her cheeks. She had to look away from his knowing stare, her eyes sinking down past his chin to land on a fresh wound on his chest. Two semicircles of teeth indents tinged with blood and haloed with swelling. Kess' blood turned to ice.

In her Heat-clouded brain, she had no memory of sinking her teeth into his pale flesh. Automatically, her fingertips reached for it but stopped before her flesh made contact, halted by some invisible barrier.

"Did I do that?" she whispered, horror frozen in the pit where her stomach used to reside.

"Well, I don't see any other horny Omega around here." His joking lilt jammed the reality in even further. Taking her hand, he closed the distance and gently laid her palm against the mark. Her hand, trapped between his chest and his palm, trembled.

Unaware, incoherent with lust and fervor, she'd done a thing that could not be undone. He'd marked her, and she'd returned the gesture.

She was well and truly caught.

The heat of the swollen flesh radiated against her palm like a living promise. She felt the truth of the mark. Like she'd bitten him and carved into her own soul in the process. Eyes closed against the swimming sensation engulfing her head, she could feel it. Could feel him, like a tiny star in her chest twinkling his name.

"I... I can *feel* you." She touched her own chest with her other hand. "*In her*e."

His teasing good humor erupted into something resembling... happiness? She'd never seen an expression like joy grace Hunter's severe features. Yet here he was, like a long-lost twin of the Alpha she knew, his face lit with delight by an actual sunbeam poking through the clouds. If she weren't a hair's breadth from hysteria, she'd be paralyzed with awe.

He cupped her cheek with a gentle, rough hand. "I'm as surprised as you, but this is..." His wide jaw flexed in a grin that heightened his handsomeness to an obscene degree, "This is more than I ever hoped for. You live in my heart now, Kess. It already belongs to you."

The star in her chest flickered and shimmered, and a wash of foreign emotion poured through her. Warm pride and satisfaction—sensations that surely, truly did not belong to her—snugged up against wary confusion and disbelief that surely did.

It had never been like this with Brock. He'd marked her, sure, and she'd returned the gesture at his emphatic urging, but she'd never felt anything at all beyond the discomfort of his bite. Certainly nothing like... this. This was something else entirely, and it scared her to death.

Horrified, Kess heaved herself away, wrenching her hand from his chest. Her eyes flew everywhere at once. Her feet, her hands, her chest—her *naked* chest—the horse, the tent, the grass, everywhere and anywhere but at the Alpha two feet in front of her.

"No," she said, backing up further. "This isn't... it wasn't supposed to be like this." Her voice pitched higher and louder, drawing attention from Cleo as a burst of foreign-feeling concern thrummed in her chest. She backed up another step, shame and dismay at her nakedness growing with every passing, near-hysterical second. As if the nudity confirmed every disturbing conclusion rattling around her brain. She was exposed, totally exposed to him. There would be no hiding from here on out. Wherever she went or whatever she did, he'd find her.

He'd find her.

"I gave up battling what's supposed or not supposed to be a long time ago." Eyes focused and sharp, Hunter took a single step and tapped his chest. "But this is. I don't know what it is, I couldn't explain it, but we're connected. You'll not be alone ever again. Your fears, your needs, your desires—they're *ours* now, to share."

All her feelings laid bare for him? Without filters, without privacy? Was nothing to be hers alone? "No, I don't want this!" the words ripped from her throat. "I don't want you!"

At this, she met his black, wild-eyed gaze. His silver corona, silly and amusing a minute ago, transformed into something menacing and ferocious. As did his taut shoulders and his chest, sucking breath after angry breath. And it was anger, all right, because she felt that too, burning a hole through her emotions like a hot coal through a piece of paper.

"It's a little late for that." His tone bulged with forced patience. "We're mates, Kess, whether you like it or not."

"Well, I *don't* like it!" Kess shook her head so hard she stumbled back another step. Regaining her balance, she pointed a tremulous finger at him. "You... I thought you were better than him, I thought... No. I'm not staying with you. Take me back to the village."

It was a wild, crazy demand. One which he'd never agree to, but it was the best her flailing brain could produce. They weren't far—a day or two's ride back? She could just go back and everything would be fine.

"You know I can't do that." He spun away, leaving her alone with her impotent rage. She watched him stalk back to the tent and yank on a pair of pants. Turning, he moved to the firepit and rekindled the flame, moving around cooking implements as if to start making food.

His attempt at normalcy left her sputtering and speechless. Was this what it was to be, then? Her, filled with abject, horrified misery, and him blithely going about his business and doing whatever he wanted while she stood around? Oh, and presumably sticking his dick in her regularly as well. If he produced a shack to imprison her, then he would have perfectly re-created her life with Brock.

Propelled by fury, she retrieved her own clothes, forcing stiff arms and legs into their appropriate garments. Once dressed, she adopted a calmness she didn't feel and approached again, lowering herself cross-legged onto the ground next to him.

"You said," she began, "that you would wait until I asked—no, begged—for your… attentions. But you didn't. You took me anyway and set off a Heat, and now all this has happened, and *I never asked for any of it.*"

"You said you were mine." Hunt stirred some oats into boiling water and cut her a grim look. "*You* said that. Not me. You gave me your mark. *You* did that—"

"While I was in Heat!"

His grizzled head shook slowly back and forth in time with the motion of his stirring spoon. "You're making a lot of excuses, Omega."

"My *name* is Kess."

Tapping the spoon against the pot, he poked at the fire, then sat back on his knees, refusing to respond to her escalating ire. "There's no place for you back at that village, and you damn well know it."

"Yes, I know. My place is with a Pack." Her inner Omega shouted caution, to not provoke him with sarcasm and spite, but she couldn't listen.

"Pack or no Pack, that group of religious zealots ain't gonna take you back, Kess." His voice sounded fatigued, even weary. "You heard the pup's mom. You think she's the only one thinking those things?" His muscled shoulder lifted in a careless gesture. "She's the only one stupid enough to say them to a Pack of Alphas, but I could read the distaste all over them."

Liar. Kess' brain spit the word like a hissing cat, but pursed lips held it back. The Alpha might tolerate some attitude, but she suspected he wouldn't tolerate being called an outright liar.

And it wasn't true. As much as she'd like to deny it— to herself, to him, to anyone who would listen—she'd acquiesced to leaving the village with the full knowledge she'd never return.

No one had even said goodbye.

Unable to summon words to counter his argument, her tongue, suddenly tacky and sour, yielded. Kess sank her forehead into her palms and rubbed at her temples. The movement both failed to soothe her aching head and, to add insult to injury, aggravated the still-healing bite.

She'd run away. Not back to the village, but somewhere else. Somewhere he wouldn't think to look.

The idea snaked through her mind, and her movements ceased, as if to hide the revelation from Hunt's keen awareness. Run away. She did it once, she could do it again. Granted, last time she didn't have a mated Alpha tracking her down, but how much harder would that make it? He slept like an absolute log. Well… sometimes he slept like a log. Usually after fucking for hours.

She'd distract him. With the only thing Alphas cared about more than themselves.

But when? And how?

She stilled her thoughts, trying to sort through the logic. They were headed west, then north, and he'd told Colt they'd meet up again in Old Tacoma. A dusty memory flickered at the edges of her thoughts. Old Tacoma… Old Tacoma… Someone had said something intriguing about Old Tacoma. But what?

The realization flared bright. The Omega sanctuary. That had been it. A trader had come through the Beta village last fall, right as Heck had started his Alpha transformation. She'd overheard the smarmy, toothless man tell Heck he ought to head to Old Tacoma and find the Omega sanctuary. He'd sneered the words with such a leering, despicable twist of his wormy lips her stomach had turned over. She'd dared not ask any further details, not wanting to betray an excessive interest in Omegas, but the idea shadowed her for days. An Omega sanctuary… a place where Omegas could be safe? It sounded too good to be true.

But now it beckoned as a source of refuge. Of hope.

And Hunter was leading her right there. All she needed to do was hide her plans from him and bide her time. Make him think she'd accepted her fate, then slip away from him once they reached Old Tacoma and find her way to the sanctuary. And if it didn't exist? Well, then she'd find another way to hide.

Plan devised, she sucked in two deep, quivering breaths, trying to regain some semblance of calm. It wasn't a great plan, but it was the best she could do. Any plan was better than being shackled to and controlled by an Alpha for the rest of her life. Brock had caught her as a naïve, blooming Omega, spiriting her away from her home and setting her up in a life she didn't know to question. *This is what Omegas do, this is what Omegas want*, he'd explained to her like she was a simple child. She'd thought she was wrong for not liking it, for not wanting it. For hating it.

But she wasn't wrong. He was wrong. *They* were wrong.

Five years she'd been on her own, and despite the struggle for survival, she'd found enjoyment and satisfaction as a member of a community, as a teacher. Not as an Omega fated to constantly produce pups year after year. No. That wasn't her.

This thing with Hunter, this distasteful bond—she didn't know what it meant, but she didn't much care. She'd had a taste of independence, and she refused to submit again.

Hunt shoved a bowl of the mushy oats at her with a grunt. Keeping her face carefully schooled, she began to eat, praying her fledgling excitement wouldn't transmit through their oppressive bond.

CHAPTER 20

Hunter

For the third time in the last hour, Hunt unclenched his jaw. This Omega posed a serious threat to his tooth enamel. How he even had tooth enamel after a hundred-and-thirty years, he sure as hell didn't know. Especially considering how rough his diet had gotten at times. He swore there were a few years there where he'd lived off little more than bark. But an overly long life and a harsh diet were nothing compared to his new, intransigent mate.

Why had anyone ever implied Omegas were sweet, docile, and constitutionally prone to submission? Nothing he'd seen with this one jived with any of that. If she had a submissive bone in her body, he'd yet to find it. And he, like an idiot, assumed once they'd made it through her Heat and exchanged mating bites, things would settle into some sort of pleasant détente.

Fat chance of that.

If anything, relations between them had deteriorated further. So much so that the prospect of bumping along twenty miles with Kess wedged between his thighs, making his cock hard while their connection in his chest blared nonstop unhappiness, drove him right off horseback. Instead he loped alongside Cleo, pacing long strides over the rugged terrain. It felt good, all things considered, to stretch his legs.

Everything hurt. Well, no, not everything, precisely. Rarely, since undergoing the Alpha transformation, did he physically ache. All those middle-aged twinges and pulls seemed to have passed him by in his modified body. But as his legs covered distances that would be unheard of in his pre-Alpha state, an unrelenting, gripping discomfort shadowed his every step. Its origin was not hard to pinpoint.

The mating bond had worked its way into his chest in some indescribable—and physiologically impossible—way. As if the Omega had stitched herself on his chest with disappearing sutures, her presence melting and absorbing into the fibers of his heart.

He'd never forget the moment she'd bitten him. Her eyes, big and glossy with blown, Heat-drunk pupils, swallowing him up as he moved inside of her. They'd been out in the open, in the sunlight, as he'd imagined the first time he saw her. Only better. Wilder. With bits of grass and twigs decorating her hair like a mystical forest fairy. Lips parted and swollen from his kisses, her eyes had shone even brighter the second before she opened her mouth and sunk her teeth right into his chest. A yell, half-surprised and half-ecstatic, had rolled out of him and into the dense forest around them as her bite triggered an epic climax.

Afterward, sated and languid, they'd cuddled by the fire, wrapped up in blankets and each other while she'd dozed, a drop of his blood staining the corner of her mouth.

He'd never known such contentment. His satisfying purr vibrated and shimmered down the bond. She'd hummed her own response, a sweet, sleepy agreement that swelled his chest with happiness. Actual, unmitigated happiness.

And then she'd woken up, and all hell broke loose. The sight of her claiming bite sent her spiraling into panic. That much was clear. Which was baffling; Hunt had never once considered she'd forged the connection with a less-than-coherent mental state, but reviewing the minutes leading up to that moment, he couldn't deny it. But what was he supposed to do? Not let her bite him? How would that even work?

Her cold rejection burned like a handful of dry ice. Acrimony simmered and snapped across the bond, impossible to discern how much came from him and how much from her. Occasionally, a tiny sprout of hope poked its head out of the bitterness, but it would be promptly pulverized.

And not by him.

They'd spent the last several days traveling in stony, brittle silence. Not much for conversation himself, he'd left her to her quiet, even if it irked him. She'd responded to direct questions and helped with the daily chores—gathering firewood, pitching the tent, foraging for food—but otherwise disengaged. Except for at night, when the confines of the tent drove them into each other's air and pasted their bodies together. He'd reached for her the first night, and she'd responded, participated, and enjoyed herself... all without a single word exchanged.

After that, he'd decided it would be better to fall asleep hard and aching than to feel the hollowness of physical connection without any trace of intimacy.

Intimacy.

The word brought a grimace to his face. One week after sniffing out an Omega, and he was pining about intimacy like a lovesick teenager. He detested his craving for her—beyond physical, a craving for her voice and smiles and conversation. And… affection.

More than anything, he wanted her to just… not hate him. Was that too much to ask? He hadn't done anything beyond what he thought typical Alpha-Omega pairs did. Granted, there was no manual, no Wiki page with instructions for navigating a relationship unlike any that had existed in before TheEnd. But he'd followed his instincts and done his best. He fed her and protected her and kept her safe. He offered her the best bits of meat and all the fresh food she could eat. He let her ride Cleo while he walked. He'd fought off an attacker. Didn't that count for anything?

Apparently not, the stinging misery in the bond reminded him.

Sniffing the salt-tinged air, he turned his thoughts to their travels. Cleo, anxious to move after pausing for Kess' Heat, trotted a quick pace over the terrain, and they'd covered a great distance. They would reach the coast before nightfall.

Even this, he'd done for her. They could've cut a path across the interior to Old Tacoma, but he'd thought she might enjoy seeing the vast Pacific. Of course, the cliffs had been his destination all along, but with a far different goal in mind.

As miserable as the strain between them felt, the bone-deep suffering that had been his constant companion for years had fully dissipated. He wasn't quite sure when, exactly, but quite possibly the moment he'd laid eyes on the pretty Omega atop his horse. Suicide appealed to him about as much as fucking a Beta woman, at this point, which was not at all. Less than zero. Bordering on aversion. His best knife, the one he'd honed and had planned to stab into his chest, he'd given to Colt to trade.

Vegetation thinned as the daylight did, and, at long last, the white-crested waves of the Pacific appeared in the distance. The sight spurred him on. They'd fall asleep to the sound of the waves.

And maybe she'd forgive him.

*

"It's beautiful, isn't it?"

Unable to bear the silence a second longer, Hunt tried again for conversation. They'd camped atop some steep cliffs and, following a simple dinner, watched the sun sink below the horizon. A soft peacefulness hummed in his chest and rippled between them for the first time in days.

The shocking riot of oranges and pinks reflected against Kess' skin and scalded him with beauty. He'd never seen anything more exquisite. Her shoulders, usually hiked up near her ears, had softened enough that he caught a glimpse of his claiming bite. Fully healed, his possessive pleasure in it embarrassed him.

Acknowledging his peace offering, Kess dipped her chin. "It's been a while since I've seen the ocean."

Her soft voice, even and untainted with bitterness and anger buoyed his hopes. Could they have a simple conversation? Establish some sense of peace?

"You've been here before?"

"Maybe? I'm not sure if I've been *here* exactly, but I…" Her lips twitched and she shot him a glance, a rapid look, and then away. "I traveled up the coast once."

Normally so taciturn, Kess dropped this tidbit, and he cradled it to his chest like a broken-winged bird, precious and fragile. If only he could keep her talking. A thousand questions sprang into his mind, yet he resisted the urge to ask them all and instead offered up a revealing tidbit of his own.

"I was born along this coast, south of here, in what was once California. But I like it here, this area. It looks as if nothing has changed. I can almost convince myself TheEnd never happened."

The Omega let out a surprised squeak and turned wide eyes to meet his. "How old *are* you?"

Hunt gazed at the water, not able to both tell the shocking truth and monitor her reaction. He'd feel it in his chest, but if she responded with horror, he didn't know what he'd do.

"Not sure, exactly," he started, cursing himself for his cowardly hedging. He wanted her to be honest with him, didn't he? "I was thirty at TheEnd." He forced himself to go on, ignoring her audible sip of air at this revelation. "It was hard to keep track of time for a while there, in the initial chaos. There were the bombs, then system failures, and then weather patterns got messed up—hurricanes, fires... Everything was about survival, and nowhere was safe.

"It took me about six months to make my way up from Mexico." He huffed a bitter laugh. "I'd been on vacation with a friend when the first bombs dropped. My friend, Jake, he... he wanted to stay there for a while, to 'wait things out.' I was going to go back and try to meet up with him, but... not sure what became of him."

Tender curiosity seeped into him. Its origin could only be Kess. "Why did you leave Mexico?"

Despite the unexpected pleasure of her interest, Hunt winced. He hadn't planned to stumble into these memories, yet if they kept the conversation going... "I was living in Seattle at the time. Jake too, actually... And my, uh..." He cleared his throat against a ball of clogging emotion. "My sister and my brother were in the area as well. I wanted to find them."

For years, he'd avoided the painful memories of that fruitless journey—traveling thousands of miles by bus, by car, and eventually by foot, only to find the decimated ruin of the city and everyone in it. Mile after mile of makeshift refugee encampments, everything coated with the sticky gray ash of destruction and stinking of sorrow. Initially he'd hoped his family members were not in one of those unhygienic, desperate places, and then he'd prayed they were.

He'd searched every camp within miles of the city. It took him over a year. By the time he gave up, he wondered if Jake had been right to remain in Mexico, along the beach where the terror hadn't yet reached. If they'd stayed together, or even traveled north together, he would've had a friend and ally rather than faced the devastation alone.

"I have a brother and sister too," Kess said softly, interrupting his regrets. "Or I did… It's been a long time since I've seen them. I tell myself they're alive and doing fine. That my mother is still alive…" Face taut with strong emotion, her words trailed away. Her eyes, rich with sadness, met his. "I miss her the most," she added, her voice nearly inaudible.

His head filled with crazy, reckless ideas like he'd find them for her. He'd take her home and reunite her with her family, and then maybe she'd…

Maybe she'd love him.

He jerked away from the thought like a hand on a hot pan. Love? Who was talking love?

"Where are they?"

"I don't know, exactly. Somewhere in the middle? I was born there." She sighed, fondness playing along her lips. "It was so beautiful… the snow in the winter, and in the summer, the sky… the open plains as far as the eye could see."

She smiled gently at this, quiet for a few minutes with her peaceful remembrances. He sat silent, giving her space, and enjoying the touch of happiness on her pretty face and the contented glow flowing through their bond.

After a moment, her gaze refocused on him, hardening again. "When Brock stole me away, we traveled for weeks.

All the way to this coast. I was barely coherent the whole time, in and out of Heats, grieving, scared, confused."

Hunt's back muscles tightened like twisting rope. He was no better than her prior Alpha. A low curse escaped his lips.

"And then what happened to you?"

Kess shook her head, fixing him with an expectant stare. "You first. What happened to you? Did you find your siblings?"

"No. I made my way north as the world fell apart. By the time I got to Seattle, or what remained of Seattle, the plagues had started." Bolstered by his desire to learn more from her, his story poured off his tongue, each word easier than the last. "I tried to… *help*—I was a doctor—but there was nothing to do except watch people die. We had no supplies, no electricity, no medicine. Eventually people stopped showing up for work at the makeshift hospital, either dead themselves or burned out, I never knew. And then one day, I couldn't get out of bed, couldn't make myself go anymore, and I quit too."

Shame gnawed at his throat, the forever scar of abandoning his post, abandoning his colleagues and the patients he could do little for. He'd run off the end of his capacities—mental, physical, emotional. Earlier in his career, colleagues had lamented something they'd dubbed compassion fatigue—a condition of feeling disconnected and numb to human suffering. But in TheEnd, he surpassed fatigue all the way to depletion. He felt nothing, cared for nothing, lived for nothing. Even the shame, when it surfaced years later, he experienced in a dull, abstract way, more of a concept than an actual feeling. Yet the suffering in the world continued around him, and his compassion had never fully returned. Another thing he'd lost, along with his family, his friends, his career, and all of his hopes and dreams.

"But you didn't get sick because you're an Alpha?"

A bitter chuckle burst out of him. Too young to remember the world before, he smiled in relief that Kess, at least, had been spared that particular pain. "There were no Alphas and Betas before TheEnd. That became apparent... later. Once folks started talking about men who were more than other men—bigger, faster, keener senses—I knew that's what I was. What I'd... become. Most Alphas running around now have been born in the AfterEnd, but something had... changed me."

He shrugged, having long ago accepted he'd never fully understand the mystery of the change in human dynamics, but he wondered. Was empathy simply not possible anymore? Had his brain and his emotions, the remaining human parts of him, been irrevocably altered along with his DNA?

Plucking a pebble, he rubbed his thumb against the grainy surface before pitching it over the cliffside. "I'll never understand it, but there it is."

She was quiet a long time, but the silence was contemplative, comforting, and their link buzzed with interest and fascination. "So you're... *a hundred and thirty years old*?"

He watched her carefully for signs of fear or disgust at this revelation. "Give or take, yeah."

Surprise lit her face at his confirmation, but no judgment tinged her curious expression. "Are there others like you?"

"Yeah, some. But I don't know how many. The remnant Alphas tend to… uh…" He grimaced. "… *annoy* each other and steer clear. A Pack usually has one, maybe two, if they can get along and not tear each other apart." He scooped up her hand in his own, tracing the lines on her palm with his fingertips. She didn't pull back, and he soaked up the small victory. "Your turn. What happened after you were stolen?"

Her head turned toward the endless ocean. "We made our way west, till we reached some Alpha lands and joined a Pack there. I think some of Brock's brothers had connections in that Pack… I don't know, honestly… but that's where we lived. There were some other Omegas around, mated pairs, but when I didn't conceive in my first few Heat cycles, Brock kept me apart from them. Wanted me to stay in our hut and 'nest.'" She spat the word with disgust. "Thought it would help get me pregnant."

Hunter's grip tightened on her hand as if, after all these years, he could haul her away from her past. Beyond the excessive bite marks, this wretched excuse for an Alpha, this Brock, had imprisoned and isolated her for *years*. He felt sick to his stomach. No wonder she hated Alphas.

"How long?" His voice was rough and gravelly. "How long did he keep you isolated like that?"

Kess tilted her head to the darkening sky as if the answer was written in the stars. "Not sure, exactly. Ten years? Fifteen?"

He didn't understand how she could speak about it with such calm when fury itself churned his guts. He pictured his poor Omega—young, sweet, innocent Kess—alone in a dwelling, staring at the same four walls, going in and out of Heats, making and re-making her nest, submitted to the Alpha over and over again. Years and years of this stilted, watery existence. He could feel her sadness, her desperation and hopelessness. Not through the bond, which hummed along steadily on her end, but through his own vivid imaginings.

As if to stay his rising agitation, Kess patted his hand gently, a sly smile tilting her lips. "That's when I taught myself to weave baskets. Out of sheer loneliness and boredom."

Hunter breathed deep, forcing himself to set aside all the whirling emotions kicked up by her story. "How did he die?"

"I don't know. He'd been complaining for weeks about headaches—terrible, splitting headaches—but there wasn't anything to be done, so... One day, the headache got even worse. He trashed our entire hut, tore everything off the walls, ripped all my baskets apart. I thought he was going to kill me, I really did." Remnants of that fear shuddered down the bond. Hunt could feel her terror like a living, breathing thing, as real as her warm hand cradled in his. "His Pack brothers held him down, and then he... convulsed? Shook for a long time, and then he was dead." She snapped her fingers. "Just like that."

"Cerebral aneurysm," he muttered. He'd never heard of an Alpha succumbing to one, but her description was amazingly consistent. Definitely a more peaceful end than that bastard of an Alpha deserved. "And you were free."

"Sort of." She wriggled her hand to free it from the death grip he'd unknowingly bestowed in response to her fear. Once released, her fingertips didn't withdraw, but danced lightly on his palm and delved between his fingers. Sweet, playful, innocent caresses that warmed him more than the fading sun on his cheeks. "We buried Brock, and I convinced the Alpha of Alphas I needed a mourning period. See... I was afraid—"

"Another Alpha in the Pack would claim you." Claim her like he had. Fresh shame poured through his bloodstream. No better than those avaricious Alphas, he'd exposed her, stolen her, claimed her, marked her... taken her away from the life she'd scratched out among the Betas. He felt awful. Dirty and wretched and selfish and horrible.

Fingers ceasing their play, her eyes dropped to her lap in wordless confirmation.

Disgusted, he leapt to his feet and stalked a few yards away. Desperate to escape the mirror she'd held up to his pitiful behavior. Over a hundred years of avoiding Omegas, and now this. The only one he'd ever wanted, would ever want, the one now tied to him body and soul, had every reason to hate his guts from here till eternity. He raked his hands through his hair, clenching handful after handful, nearly ripping it out by the roots.

His gaze spilled over the cliff, taking in the rocks below and the ocean beyond. Like a massive wave flattening a sandcastle, an idea slammed into him.

This had been his plan.

Rocks. Waves. Knife. Death.

It could still be his plan. He didn't want this plan, but he could do it. He could do what that bastard dead Alpha never could.

He could set her free.

CHAPTER 21

Kess

Hunt paced the cliff's sharp edge, waves of agitation rolling off him. The unwitting spell she'd fallen under had been broken. A quiet evening, an open sky, and a salty sea breeze was all it had taken to seduce her into revealing truth after truth of her closely guarded history. For days, riding atop Cleo, escape occupied her mind: when she would slip away, what she'd need to survive, how she would avoid him. And now here she was, all thoughts of the Omega sanctuary forgotten as her reservations crumbled one by one. A few simple questions, and she granted him a tour of her secrets. It was as if the bond itself had lured her into this intimacy.

It wanted her acquiescence. It *longed* for it, and she'd obliged. Sublimely, carelessly contented as the feelings of openness and mutual acceptance ebbed and flowed between the two of them. Demonstrating, once again, the realness of this connection.

All those years with Brock, it had never been like this. He'd bit her, over and over, trying to forge whatever this joining was. Trying to force a connection and blaming her for its failure.

It had never worked. Not until now. Not until Hunter.

Hunter, who now prowled the precipice like a territorial cat, grabbing angry, painful-looking fistfuls of hair. Something had come over him, yet she couldn't discern what. The bond hissed and crackled with a mess of emotions too convoluted to parse. Too many, too intense, too fast. His turmoil became her turmoil, and she couldn't find her way through to the other side.

Unsure what else to do, she stood and approached his side, grabbing his hand to cease the worrisome pacing. "Hunter, what is it? What's going on?"

His eyes, usually so pale and clear and intelligent, turned on her with a ferociousness that made her flinch. His hair, mussed by his frantic attentions, stuck out in all directions.

With a grim set to his mouth, he grasped her upper arms in his immense hands. "I'll do it." His voice, gruff and guttural, raked across her ears. "I'll set you free, Kess. You can take Cleo and go…" His eyes left hers to circle the campsite, the ocean, the sky. He gave a helpless shrug. "Wherever you want to go. Back to that village, or find a new one."

What? Dark spots bobbed before her eyes as her every thought collided. She blinked and blinked again, scrambling to understand. What was happening? The Alpha who'd declared, *we're mates, Kess, whether you like it or not*, proposing to let her go? But why? Why now? It made no sense.

Shaking her head, Kess tried to step away, but his hands only tightened around her further. "What are you talking about?"

Chest heaving with monstrous, heavy breaths, he explained, "You said it yourself: you didn't want this. You don't want me." His voice broke on the word me, and the raw anguish nearly split her in two. But why? They might be connected, but she didn't care for this Alpha. "You never had a choice—that's what you said. That's what I'm giving you, Kess. My gift to you: a choice."

Her heart raced, pounding against her chest in a riot of inexplicable fear and opportunity. She could be free, truly? He'd just... let her go? It couldn't be true. It simply couldn't.

"I don't understand. What's the choice? I take Cleo and leave you here? What... What will you do?"

His eyebrows lifted as if he couldn't believe she was asking this question. "Well, I'll be dead, of course."

Dead. The word echoed in her ears as if he'd shouted it over the cliffside.

Dead. Hunter would be dead.

One blink and she saw it all: Hunter's broken, unmoving body plastered against the rocks, beaten and jostled by the unrelenting surf. Chiseled jawline slackened and limp in a death mask. Beautiful silver hair dark with blood and clinging to his handsome, lifeless face.

Nausea launched up her throat. Kess jerked from his grip to stumble away, a choking sensation gripping and forcing her to draw harsh, insufficient sips of air. "Dead? Why would you be dead?"

"Well, I'll kill myself," he said simply, gesturing over the cliff. "I hate the AfterEnd. No reason to stay alive for another hundred years. I had it all worked out. Of course, that changed when I met you." An affectionate smile kindled on his lips before he continued to dispassionately, insanely explain, "But I can see now that I shouldn't have claimed you. It… It hurt you too much, and if this is the only way to make it right, then…"

He gestured again at the sheer drop, as if that, indeed, were any kind of solution.

Her chest rattled and lurched, the bond desperate and out of control as desolation roared through her body. Terror seeped into her very bones. The things she'd lamented—choice, freedom, agency—withered and paled in the stark light of a separation. She wanted those things. She did! Didn't she?

"No!" she barked, closer with each second to a full-on, hysterical panic. "Offering to kill yourself isn't giving me a choice. That's no choice, Hunt, that's… that's blackmail!" Pulse hammering in her ears, she clutched at her chest as if stoppering a wound. "What about this? What about the bond? *What happens to the bond, Hunt*?"

His shoulders slumped, the fervor propping up his plan deflating. "I'd let you go free and clear, Kess, I would,"— he lowered himself to his knees at her feet—"but I don't think the bond would let you get far, and I'm not sure I can promise to not come after you. Death is the only way I can think of to truly let you go, baby."

All the blood in her body simultaneously rushed into and out of her head. Sick and dizzy, her emotions swarmed, both her own—panic, revulsion, dismay—and Hunt's—certainty, resignation, resolve.

But it was the baby that destroyed her remaining control.

Kess squeezed her eyes shut and shook her head. "No. No, no, *no*. That's… That's not… I can't…" Clenching her fists, she gazed into his sad, subdued eyes and forced herself not to scream as she imagined the clear blue dulled and unfocused, their light forever darkened. "You can't ask me to kill you. I won't do it. I *won't*."

With a pitying, patient look, Hunt unfurled one of her fists and pressed its limp digits to his cheek, as simultaneously scruffy and soft as him. "It's not murder, Kess; it's *sacrifice*. It's righting a wrong." He brought the hand to his lips. "Let me do this for you. Let me try to fix what every Alpha has done to fuck up your beautiful, precious life. You deserve a life, *a real life*. One not tied to me."

She was going to vomit. Whatever they'd eaten for dinner—at this point she couldn't even say—heralded its return. It was perverse, the way he repeated her own beliefs back to her, the way he held them out on a plate as if she could just pick them up and take a bite. Take a bite and poison herself with the knowledge she'd cursed him to a violent, unnatural death. It didn't matter one single bit that she believed he had truly intended to end his own life before meeting her; his life wasn't his own anymore.

Part of him lived in her. These past days of traveling together—even as she resented it, resented him—his presence beat a steady, reassuring pulse inside her. But now that thread arced and writhed, transmitting pain at the mere thought of cleaving the bond. Surely, he felt it on his side of the tether. It had to be as terrible, as paralyzing, as catastrophic as it was to her.

It didn't matter if she'd wanted it or not, if she'd accepted it or not, if she even liked him or not, because he'd lodged inside of her, and she knew she'd never be free. And the worst part was *he* knew it too.

Hence his unhinged solution.

Lightheaded, Kess dropped to her knees and braced her palm on her forehead, taking in breath after unsteady breath. Large, warm arms enclosed around her and brought her cheek to his firm, fragrant chest. Hunt's woodsy scent permeated her senses and soothed her from the inside out. And then he began to purr. Deep and rhythmic and meant only for her. Tears bubbled in the corners of her eyes.

How could her captor break her heart with his offer of freedom?

He shushed and whispered and held her even tighter.

CHAPTER 22

Kess

Kess had heard a gunshot only once in her life. An Alpha in Brock's Pack had a gun, and a very limited number of bullets. Drunk and rowdy one night, he'd made a big show of trying to shoot—and spectacularly miss—a propped-up target. Huddled in her solitary hut, nursing a fresh bite wound, she'd not participated in that evening's revelry, but she'd bolted from her dwelling to follow that horrific, ringing noise to its source. Her frantic response to the noise gave new meaning to the expression "gone off like a shot."

No gunshot penetrated the ocean's hearty susurrus, but Kess' eyes sprang open as if one had. Her body levered upright, primed for action, something telling her—no, insisting—that Something Was Wrong.

Hunt's scent lingered in the tent, as did the complex blend of their mating the night before. They'd huddled together at the cliffside until she'd stopped crying, and then he'd carried her back to the tent and kissed her tears and all other thoughts away until she'd cooed and purred and climaxed in his arms. Exhausted and emotionally wrung out, she'd surrendered to deep, inert sleep.

But he was gone. Her foggy brain tripped over itself to orient to the confused, harsh awakening. There was danger somewhere, but what, exactly? Pulling on her clothes,

Kess pushed past the tent flaps and scanned the cliffside and the riverbank for signs of the Alpha. Even without a visual of him, the origin of the danger clarified and presented itself.

It was coming from *inside* her, from the bond. It clawed at her, an unhappy, tortured thing.

Oh God. Had he…?

Had he not waited for her answer to his proposal? Had he gone ahead and tried to end things? Surely she would know if he were dead, wouldn't she? The fact she still felt something, albeit something awful, in the bond had to mean he was still alive. Right?

Spurred by this thought, Kess tore to the precipice, sickened at what she might find as one phrase repeated over and over in her mind like a prayer.

He can't be dead.

Stumbling, frantic, nauseous, she scanned the rocks below for a huge Alpha body. He couldn't be dead.

He was there.

Not prostrate and broken on the rocks, but perched a short distance away, elbows on his knees, hands cradling his face, distress written in every line of his posture. The discomfort in her chest flashed in recognition, a single beat of reinforced connection. Hunt's head turned in her direction, eyes connecting from fifty yards and a steep cliff away, and relief rolled through her muscles one by one.

Heaving a giant sigh, she noticed the serpentine trail winding its way down to the water's edge. Worried he'd hurl himself into the ocean before she could stop him, she charged toward the path, her steps hurried and sloppy as she slipped and skidded down. Somehow she knew he wouldn't harm himself in front of her, but the fear occupied a hard, cold place in her belly, so terrifying she refused to take her eyes off him the entire treacherous journey.

He held her attention, not looking away, but not rising to meet her either. Too content—or too discontented?—to rise to help or even halt her progress. Such a contrast to his every action in the past week, forever attuned and focused on her and her comfort exclusively. She'd taken it for granted—his automatic, unassuming kindness.

Obscured by the Alpha possessiveness she loathed on principle, confused by the heights of pleasure when they mated, miserable with her burgeoning escape plans, Kess had failed to appreciate the depths of his unwavering care and concern. All the way to his desperate offer to end his fucking life for no reason other than to give her a chance at happiness. Not even a certainty or guarantee of happiness, but a sad, pathetic, unlikely chance. He'd throw his life away on a thin hope, on a barely-there whisper of a prayer.

And doom them both.

"No," she said to herself, picking her way off the trail and onto the soggy, sinking sand. And then again, louder as she stomped toward the Alpha ten yards away. "No. That's my choice, no." The sucking sand hindered her steps. Frustrated, Kess kicked off her loosely laced boots to finish the distance on cold feet, tilting her head up to meet his brokenhearted gaze. "You won't kill yourself, Hunter. I won't allow it."

Something shifted in his pale eyes, and a sprinkle of amusement crept around his firm, gorgeous lips. "Is that right?"

Her Omega nature sounded a word of caution. To not disagree with the Alpha, to not anger or upset the Alpha, to pacify and comfort the Alpha. But she ignored it, firm in her belief that *this* Alpha would accept her assertion of control. At this moment, he would. He had to.

"Yes, that's right." Her voice became surer, and she laid a hand on his thigh. "You won't do anything to harm yourself. I forbid it—today, tomorrow, or any other day, and I don't want to hear another single word about it. Do you understand me, Hunter?"

A teasing glint sharpened the corners of his eyes. "You sound like a schoolteacher."

"I am a schoolteacher. Or I was…" Her shoulder jumped. "It doesn't matter now. Now I'm well and truly yours. Your Omega, your mate. And if that's the only thing I am, that is plenty."

The words tumbled from her lips, overflowing with emotion and sentiment and truth. She'd left the ridge above not wanting him to die, not wanting to have blood on her hands for her own miserable existence, but her feelings had shifted in the descent. She didn't want him to die, not for her own guilt or moral purity, but because she wanted him by her side.

Hunt was right. AfterEnd was a wretched, horrible place full of danger and injustice and so little succor, it was a wonder anyone survived. But, without being fully aware of it, she'd found something of value in Hunter, something precious and irreplaceable and life-affirming. Something she didn't want to give up.

Something she couldn't live without.

Amusement fell off his face as it crumpled into an expression of such poignant, affectionate sincerity, it made her breath come short. In one smooth motion, he slid off the rock and gathered her in his arms.

"You're much more than that." She barely picked out his deep, resonant voice above the pounding surf mere feet away. But she heard all the complicated emotions tucked inside the admission as it vibrated in the space between their chests and the connection therein.

Brimming with tenderness, her hands drifted up, cupping the strong lines of his Alpha jaw. "I don't know you, Hunter. Not really. But… what I do know is how kind and caring you are underneath all this… *gruff*."

He enveloped one of her wrists, pressing it firm to his face. His eyes closed as he nuzzled his cheek further into her palm, brow furrowed with serious, concentrated bliss. Her newfound affection swelled around her insides, taking up more and more space, as much space as possible in this simple action of allowing and accepting her comfort. Comfort he craved as much as she did, Alpha or not.

"I don't…" He stopped to clear his throat, "I don't deserve you, Kess. I've done nothing in my life to d—"

"You have." She raised up on her tiptoes to snake a hand into his hair, fisting the soft strands to emphasize her point. "You *survived*. All these years, you survived. Who would've saved me from Van, if not for you?"

"Who would've stolen you from the village, if not me?" he countered, unconvinced.

Kess shook her head softly. "I was on borrowed time in the village. Living on the periphery, scratching out an existence, telling myself I belonged. They tolerated me, but I never belonged. Sooner or later some Pack would've come by, and then…"

"Someone else would've robbed you of your freedom," he finished euphemistically. "I don't know that I'm much better."

"Are you going to lock me up and not let me out till I conceive? Are you going to bite me over and over, causing pain and never-ending wounds to mark your claim? Are you going to burn my books and refuse to let me read?"

His eyes lit. "You have books?"

"Yes, buried at the bottom of my pack." She giggled. All those times he'd handled her pack, how could he not have noticed the sharp, bulky edges? She swept a thumb across his broad cheekbone and continued, undeterred, "You didn't rob me of anything. I don't know if an Omega's place is always with a Pack. My mother… if she was an Omega, I didn't know it. She never told me anything. But from what I can piece together,"—she inhaled and let loose a sigh—"*my* place is with *you*. And, in the middle of this mess of a world, we can care for each other, Hunt, and maybe that's a gift we shouldn't take for granted."

"You're sure?" He rested his forehead against hers, warm breath fanning her ocean-cooled skin. "There's no going back on this, Kess. We make this promise now, and that's it. You're with me. Truly."

To her surprise, nothing in her balked at this. Outside of her awareness, maybe she'd accepted Hunter days ago when she'd placed that bite. Accepted him in her life as easily as in her body. Accepted him in her heart as well as her bed. Accepted him in a way she'd never accepted Brock. Brock, for whom she'd only ever felt resignation and dismay at his determination to force their pairing. As if he could pound a square peg into a round hole.

Whereas Hunter... Hunter was the just-right peg. Made for her, and her alone.

Kess drifted her lips over the corner of his mouth and whispered against his skin, "Truly."

*

As if they belonged to another person, Hunter's hands rolled the bedding and stuffed the packs and gathered the supplies. All morning, since they had returned to the campsite, his capable hands went through the motions while his head and body swam with a strange and novel feeling.

Joy.

Actual, unmitigated joy.

My place is with you. Kess' words, rich with feeling and truth, sang in his thoughts and surrounded him in a cloud of bliss. Contentedness pumped through his veins and lightened every thought, every movement, every sensation. He felt awake in a way he hadn't in... decades. No, not awake, necessarily... *awakened.* Like everything was new, like he was new. His Alpha body, often so big and distasteful, felt settled and serene, as if everything had fallen into its exact right place and nothing would disturb his peace ever again.

He almost didn't know how to act.

Hunter huffed a small laugh, shaking his head at himself. He didn't know how to act. Hunter, the Alpha of Alphas who'd survived a hundred years in the AfterEnd by his wits and grit, didn't know how to act. Didn't know how to be happy.

As they'd done over and over all morning, as if drawn to the source, his eyes drifted to Kess. She pulled a wide-toothed comb through her damp locks, the spirals forming one by one under her attentions. She loved her hair. *He* loved her hair. He loved her.

So fucking much.

Her eyes, brown and warm, caught on his. "Something funny?"

His cheeks split into a grin at her playful suspicion. "Nothing. Just thinking about how wild this all is. I still…" He ducked his head with a sudden shyness. "I can't believe you're mine."

She lowered the comb from her hair, tenderness written in every line of her face, and took a slow exhale. "I'm sorry it had to come to that, Hunter. That you felt you had to… do *that*… for me."

"No." He shook his head forcefully. "I was wrong to not consider your perspective. I saw myself and thought, 'why is she so upset? I'm nothing like the dead Alpha.' But how would you know that?" He moved the few feet to her side and cupped her jaw, stroking a thumb over a smooth, rounded cheek. "I've been on my own for so long, I forgot how to care for others, forgot what empathy looked like. I certainly forgot what it felt like, what it *feels* like." Raising his other hand, he guided her lips to his for a soft kiss and a promise. "But I'm going to remember. For you, for the Pack, from here on out. I promise, Kess."

Water glistened on her lower lids, glossing her big eyes till they shined like sun-kissed amber. "Oh, Hunter," she sighed. "You're not the monster you think you are."

Feeling pressure in his chest, as if his heart itself swelled and threatened to overflow its bony cage, as if all of the long-suppressed emotions rushed out of every hidden crevice and cranny in his soul, his mouth stumbled, his tongue fumbling for a suitable response to the undeserved faith she had in him and her never-ending generosity. Unable to find one, he held her gaze, letting everything he couldn't say show on his face.

With a sweet, gentle smile, she wove her fingertips through his beard and up to his scalp. Then she kissed him again. And again.

CHAPTER 23

Hunter

They rolled into Old Tacoma around midday in the midst of a spring rain. Pissing raindrops too small to feel individually banded together to run down his face and beard in slow, irritating drips. The entire outer layers of their clothes were soaked through, and Hunt's only thought these last few hours was getting Kess somewhere dry and warm.

Oblivious to the rain, a bustling crowd went about their business in the central market. Ubiquitous signs of electricity indicated the reestablishment of power progressed at a rapid pace in this part of the world. On his previous visit three years prior, electricity remained sparse and strictly conserved for nighttime hours. Now, in the dreary, overcast day, lights buzzed and flickered from market stalls and shop windows. He even saw an old-school neon beer sign and, despite the cold and damp, amusement tugged the corner of his lip.

Along with the lights, Hunt noted the mix of Alphas and Betas passing through the burgeoning city. Certainly, in the early days of the AfterEnd, the larger and physically intimidating Alphas attracted overt stares and shrinking away responses from the more prevalent Betas. But, recognizing the value of attracting commerce of all kinds, the area's leaders designed Old Tacoma as a "neutral zone" in the new frontier.

And it appeared to be working. Alphas dotted the crowds, usually a head or a full head-and-shoulders above the Beta masses. Some Alpha-Omega pairs, recognizable by their twin bite marks or the Omega's pregnant state, circulated, as did some Alpha-Beta pairings as well. Of the three dynamics, Omegas remained the rarest and he'd never criticize an Alpha for taking a Beta mate if the alternative wasn't available. That being said, he couldn't help feeling smug at the lush, gorgeous Omega sat in front of him.

Hunt nudged Cleo to merge into the teeming traffic, directing the horse from behind Kess' swiveling head as she also took it all in. Off to their right, Hunt pointed to a bath house advertising hot showers. A barber and braiding salon occupied space next to the bathhouse, sort of a one-stop, grooming assembly line. Kess nodded enthusiastically, and her wide, excited grin sparked a matching smile of his own. When was the last time he'd been completely clean-shaven? Hunt ran a palm up his overgrown neck and face, imagining gliding a shaved, smooth cheek against Kess' delicate inner thighs. He shifted slightly in the saddle, adjusting his seat as the idea awakened some very enthusiastic parts of his body.

Kess angled her head back. "Do you think your Pack is already here?"

"We'll head to Mindy's and see. It's a restaurant and lodging house," he explained to her puzzled face. "And they have stables for the horses. If the Pack is here, that's where they'll be."

Kess' finely etched brows arched. "A restaurant? A real one?"

"Would I lie to you, baby?" Unable to repress a smile, Hunt planted a kiss on one of her perfect brows. "You hungry?" An answering rumble emanated from her stomach, forceful enough to flutter against his hand. He chuckled. "I'll take that as a yes. Food first, then bath."

The last few days of travel to Old Tacoma, Hunt cracked more smiles than he had in the fifty years prior. His laugh, once as rusty as abandoned cars in the AfterEnd, spilled out of him as easy as a sharp word for his Pack. Since their agreement by the ocean shores, he'd never spent three happier days. Not just in the AfterEnd, but in his entire life. Almost as if once Kess committed to staying, all the tumblers fell into place and unlocked... something. He couldn't explain it, but it was good.

She was good, her smile wider, her gaze softer, her kisses sweeter. In fact, he embarrassed himself with his besotted detailing of all of her likes, dislikes, and indifferences. She loved fresh foods—nuts, berries, bitter watercress, and dandelion greens—but wouldn't turn her nose up at anything offered, and he fed her every chance he got. She'd shared her paltry library and shyly asked if he would enjoy listening to her read aloud. Emotion had thickened his throat and struck him dumb at the request. All he could manage was a terse nod of assent and was unduly rewarded for the thin reply. The absolute pleasure of her rich, throaty voice bringing the words to life was a gift beyond his worth. Angling his head to the side, he brushed a kiss against her soft, damp cheek and felt the answering curl of her smile under his lips. Being indoors and dry would be a relief, but he had enough warmth brewing inside of him to withstand an arctic snowstorm.

Mindy's, located on the periphery of the Old Tacoma during his last visit, now found itself with neighbors in every direction. A bar had sprung up next door and music spilled out into the street, along with rowdy shouts of revelry. Across the way, a general store sold and traded goods, a steady stream of patrons going in and out.

After situating Cleo in the stable, they made their way to the front entrance of Mindy's. Kess clung to him throughout, clearly anxious in the unfamiliar setting. Not that he minded keeping her glued to his side. Hunt's chest swelled with pride as eyes alighted on him and his beautiful Omega. For once in his life in the AfterEnd, he didn't mind the excess attention.

At Mindy's, Hunt scanned the loitering crowd on the front porch, alert for indications of unrest or menace or any familiar faces of his Pack. The mixed group appeared friendly enough, but long years in the AfterEnd had taught him extra vigilance never went wasted. Yet most of the customers blended together—brown, water-streaked faces, hair in various states of wet, and clothes soaked through. No one giving off any kind of questionable vibe. He allowed himself to relax, but just slightly.

After some jostling and weaving, Hunter settled them at a table far from the front door. No signs of any his Pack brothers, but he'd ask around once they'd had a chance to fill their bellies.

Kess' raised voice caught his attention. "Where will we sleep tonight?"

Hunt acknowledged her question with a nod, but went back to scanning the room. "Here, if Mindy has room for us. If not, it looks like there are a few more lodging options since I was last here." He threw her a reassuring smile. "We'll find somewhere."

"I guess we can always bunk with Cleo in the stables. Seemed dry in there, at least."

Hunt barked a laugh. Satisfied the room was safe, he centered his attention on his Omega. "Yes, but who could sleep with the smell? Those stables are overdue for some cleaning out."

She grinned. "It can't be worse than a Pack of Alphas."

"Are you trying to give me a message, Omega?" Amused, Hunt made a show of sniffing at his armpits as if judging for himself. Overall, he wasn't exactly fresh, but not as bad as he had been at times in his past.

Kess laughed. "If you would listen, I said a *Pack*, not you. You smell…" Here her nostrils flared, as if she sought his scent in the musty room, her eyes hooding in response to whatever she'd perceived. A pink tongue snuck out and touched her curvy bottom lip, same as it had that morning when she'd sucked him deep and licked a drop of spilled seed. His groin tightened with the vivid recollection. "Perfect," she finished. "You smell like mine."

The heat in her gaze blazed like a fresh log scattering sparks on the fire. Leaning forward, Hunt snuck a palm between her soft thighs, spreading them slightly and wandering up until his small finger gently nudged her center. Her shiver awakened his cock further.

"Be careful with talk like that, Omega. I'm liable to bend you over this table and show you who belongs to whom."

She raised an imperious brow. "What about dinner?"

He angled closer to nip at the delicate skin of her neck, his voice dropping to a growl. "Dinner can wait."

"Is that right?" she breathed, arching the fragrant skin closer to his mouth in a dual request for more kisses and a show of sweet submission. He'd been kidding about fucking her on the table, although suddenly it didn't seem as fanciful as it had been when he'd said it.

He hummed an agreement as his teeth captured her earlobe and tugged it. "Maybe once here to take the edge off, just until I get you into an actual bed."

"Hunter!" A shrill voice pierced the hazy arousal fog. With a final lick, he pulled away and faced Mindy in her brusque, cantankerous glory. "Get yourself under control! You're giving half the men in here hardons, and Lord knows none of my girls want to deal with that."

To emphasize her point, she jerked a thumb over her shoulder to indicate both the attention they'd drawn from Alphas and Betas alike, and also her furiously working kitchen staff separated from the room by only a half-wall. At his glance, every curious pair of eyes scurried away and hyper-focused on the beers in front of them.

"How are you, Mindy?" he asked smoothly, sparing a look at the older Beta woman who gave this place its name and kept it in line. More gray touched her hair since his last visit, but her rounded cheeks still held a rosy glow of youth. Either that, or it was the heat from slinging drinks and food in the humid room. Electricity or no, they were still years away from reinventing central air.

"Same as ever." She cut a glance toward Kess. "Who's this, then? Did you find yourself an Omega after all these years?"

Grinning broadly, Hunt made the introductions, bursting with pleasure at introducing Kess as his matcd Omega.

Apparently satisfied, Mindy rained a sunny smile on Kess. "I've met my share of Alphas in this place, and most of them aren't worth a spit, but this one's a good one."

Kess' eyes rested on him, her gaze relaxed and open and full of so much trust, emotion threatened to choke him all over again. Holding Kess' hand, he exchanged some small talk with Mindy, catching up on local developments and inquiring as to available rooms for the night and any appearance of his Pack brothers. Despite the jammed restaurant, Mindy promised a room equipped with an actual bed. With a squeeze of Kess' thigh, Hunter almost demanded to go there posthaste and damn the dinner to hell.

"Hunt," Kess said, interrupting his vivid imaginings. "Is there somewhere I can... uh..." Her voice softened. "...relieve myself?"

"Yeah, of course," Mindy answered, pointing to the back door. "We've got latrines out back. Both male and female. You two want some dinner?"

"We do," Hunt said and turned to Kess. "Let me finish ordering and I'll take you, baby. You got any beer, Mindy?"

Kess tapped his hand resting on her thigh. "I can go alone. It's outside?" she asked Mindy.

Mindy pointed a pencil toward the rear exit. "Sure, sugar, right out the back door. They've been upgraded since the last time you were here," she said to Hunter. "Got separate ones for ladies and gents now. With doors and everything, real nice."

Hunter frowned, weighing letting his Omega go alone versus risking an independence-asserting lecture from his spirited mate. He studied Kess' face for any sign of anxiety. "You sure?"

"I'm not going to get lost out the back door, Hunter," she said, smiling as she planted a kiss on his cheek. "I'll be right back, and I'd like some beer too, please."

He gave her thigh an affectionate squeeze as she rose from her chair. "Anything you want, baby."

CHAPTER 24

Kess

Kess' heart pitter-pattered in her chest like the rain dripping off the buildings. Skipping between mud puddles, she crossed the small alley to the latrines Mindy described. She'd never been in a structure designed for human waste, but she'd read about *bathrooms* and *washrooms* and *restrooms* and *ladies' rooms* in books. The cramped space with a hole in the ground hardly counted as room, and the stench was anything but restful, but her excitement at the new experience offset her anxiety at being alone in the world without Hunt by her side.

She'd passed through Old Tacoma briefly after her escape. Intent on avoiding notice, she'd clung to the outer areas and avoided the busier markets where Alphas and other Omegas might make note of her. Even with her dim recollections, she recognized the city had grown quite a lot.

So this experience, in the heart of Old Tacoma with Hunter, was all new. She'd never been around so many people. Everywhere she turned in this strange, bustling place, she saw people. Alphas, Omegas, Betas all intermixed and going about their business with hardly a passing glance at one another. She had absolutely no idea what their business even was, but they moved with intent and purpose. It was all she could do to stick close to

Hunter's side so as not to be washed away in the coursing river of humanity.

Nonetheless, while she was happy at Hunter's side, the opportunity to strike out on her own—even if only to relieve herself—thrilled her. He had been watchful and protective from the moment he'd stormed into her shack, but ever since their cliffside reckoning, Hunt had become utterly devoted and unflinchingly attentive. They'd had more than one chat about her ability to take care of herself when his solicitousness bordered on the absurd.

Any possible thing, no matter how small, that might add to her comfort spurred him to action. Despite sleeping rough, eating from a mix of Hunter's dried stores and what could be trapped or gathered as they traveled, she'd never had a belly so full. Every few hours, Hunt pressed food into her hands, his not-so-subtle message he thought she needed to eat. So long accustomed to starvation and ignoring hunger pains, a few times he'd explained her belly had been complaining. She didn't notice, but he did.

And at night… his concern never waned. Past the intensity of her Heat, and with little else to do after a day's worth of travel, their matings slowed to a lazy, yet thrilling cadence, and nowhere was his consideration on more delicious display than in their bed roll. Kess buttoned up her pants with a wry smile teasing her lips. Maybe his constant feeding was calibrated to ensure she had enough energy for their nighttime activities. Not that she'd complain.

Stepping outside the stinking latrine, she used a waterspout to wash her hands, musing about what Mindy's might offer by way of food. Hopefully something hot and fresh and novel to warm her belly.

"Ava? Ava, is that you?" A man's deep voice cut into her thoughts, his frantic tone jabbing a warning up her spine. An Alpha charged across the deserted lane, his eyes gleaming with fervent intent and focused entirely on her.

Heartbeat thundering in her ears, Kess hastened a step toward Mindy's back door, her foot twisting in a puddle up to her ankle. Hot pain shot up her leg at the unnatural flex of her joint. She collapsed and struck her opposite knee on a rock. She cried out at the dual torment, rubbing at her knee as cold puddle water soaked into her pants, finding fibers even the hours of relentless rain hadn't discovered.

Strong hands gripped her shoulders and hauled her to her feet. "Ava! Oh my God! I didn't mean to scare you, honey, I'm so sorry."

Like all Alphas, he was large and held her trembling arms in a tight grip. Much like Hunter, her eyes only reached his mid-chest, but she tilted her head up, forcing words through the fear in her chest.

"I don't know you. I'm not Ava—"

"It's okay, honey," he said, his crazed eyes softening with pity. "I've got you now."

The Alpha was a stranger, and the way he spoke with such familiarity scared her. In some ways, he resembled Hunter, with his lighter skin and pale, floppy hair. Only unlike Hunter, his sopping, matted hair hadn't been combed for ages. A scraggly beard covered his face, overgrown and dirty, and his scent seared her nose, sharp with the tang of unwashed Alpha and the sickly-sweet note of rot. But most terrifyingly, it was layered with the heady scent of sexual need. Her eyes watered as the odor overtook her other senses.

Ignoring her words, with a quick movement, he scooped her up and braced her against his chest. Long, determined strides carried them beyond the alley and behind the buildings before Kess could get another word out.

"No, stop! Please put me down!" She pushed against his chest and attempted to wiggle her body out of his iron grip. "I'm not Ava. I'm Kess! I'm a mated Omega! My Alpha will kill you!"

To her words and struggles, he only held her tighter, adjusting his hold to pin her arms to her sides.

"Of course you're mated," he said with an insane chuckle. "To me. Oh, I've missed you so much. Everything's going to be all right now. I've got you, honey, okay?"

To her absolute disgust, he hiked her body farther up and dug his nose into her hair, sucking in a loud, dramatic lungful and bringing her even closer to his eye-watering stench. It was so strong it distracted her from her whirling, scrambling thoughts.

With an empty belly and muscles already fatigued from a soggy day on horseback, her fruitless struggles barely drew his attention as he made quick work of spiriting her away from Mindy's. Away from Hunt! She didn't know what to do.

Quickly they passed behind the cluster of buildings and slipped down a nearby road, where the crowds thinned and the lights were less plentiful. She wiggled and strained, a steady stream of pleas coming out of her mouth, but no one they passed, Alpha or Beta, took heed of her. In the overcast dusk, she could barely make out distinct faces of passersby as they huddled against the relentless drizzle. A group of Alphas, loud and drunk and reeking of sex, smirked at her cries for release, no doubt convinced by only a glance that he was, in fact, her Alpha on his way to discipline his disobedient Omega.

Fuck! She hated them all. So fucking much.

And where was Hunt? The bond in her torso hummed a happy, contented thrum from Hunter. She could almost see him relaxing at the table, his foot propped on a chair and beer in hand as he waited for her to return.

Only she wasn't returning! She was moving farther away from him. Could he feel her? Could he feel her distress? And where was this Alpha taking her? She didn't know this place, these streets, these landmarks. He made so many quick, sharp turns, she wouldn't even be able to find her way back should she get away.

But it didn't matter; she had to try. Frantic, Kess thrashed in his hold, kicking and bucking, slamming her head into his solid pectorals. Her twisted ankle complained at the activity. Would she even be able to walk? To run?

"Let me go, you motherfucker!"

A dark foreboding wrapped itself around her muscles and froze them in place, the struggle against an unmovable Alpha body rising up from her memory like a specter—

pinned against Brock as he'd dragged her away from the lake, running and lengthening the distance between her friends in long Alpha strides, darting to and fro to obscure their path in case anyone dared to follow.

Had anyone followed? She'd never know. All she'd known was a determined sprint through the forest, and then she was dropped on the ground, her bottoms torn away so she could be mounted before a scream even reached her lips. All the while her mind and her body warred with each other, her body sending out signals of happy acquiescence in the presence of an Alpha's attention while her mind spun itself sick grappling to understand what was happening to her.

That was different, at least. Neither her brain nor her body wanted this Alpha. It was as if all of her cells recoiled at once, and a deep, cold shudder racked her body. Her thrashing turned to violent, uncontrollable shaking. This caught the Alpha's attention, but he never slowed as the city fell silent behind them.

"It's okay, Ava. Hang on, honey, we're almost there." He donned a soothing tone as if speaking to a child, despite the fact that his inexorable grasp never eased.

Something was very wrong with this Alpha. His deranged eyes, his deafness to her appeals, the way he couldn't discern from her scent she was mated to another. She'd always understood that mated Omegas carried a mark of their possession not only on their bodies, but in their scent. Even Hunter had recently remarked that her bouquet had changed into something richer, more complex and more alluring. He'd said it deepened her appeal to him, but would be a deterrent for other Alphas.

Yet this one either did not discern it or chose to ignore it, or even worse—and the option she feared the most—he believed the evidence of her mated status was due to him. He leered down at her, his Alpha desire odor thickening the air between them and cramping her nauseous stomach to the point of pain.

"These wet clothes aren't good for you," he continued to croon. "I'll warm you up, no problem."

"I'm not Ava," she stuttered out between chattering teeth, her jaws aching with the effort to control them. "I'm not Ava. You made a mistake."

Desperate and shaking, not knowing what else to do, Kess screamed in her heart. She screamed across the bond, working with all her inner strength to disrupt Hunter's contentment. How long had it been since she'd left to use the latrine? Wasn't he noticing she hadn't come back? It seemed like hours she'd been imprisoned by this maniac, but maybe it had only been minutes.

Hunter! Where are you? Help me!

Away from the lighted streets, darkness and eerie quiet covered everything. The Alpha had taken her to the periphery of the old city, a sight more typically recognizable from her prior travels. Abandoned cars and trucks on former roadsides, piles of soggy, decaying refuse on the ground, empty buildings with dark, shattered windows gaping like the ever-open mouths from her nightmares. A wasteland, indeed. A short walk from the industry surrounding Mindy's, and she was back in AfterEnd ruination.

Ear-splitting squeals and the grinding of solidified gears jarred Kess from her recollections. With her body secured against the stinking Alpha, he used his shoulder to nudge open the yawning gate of a large, shadowy vehicle. She blinked, trying to clear the fog of her fear and the wet from her eyes to discover what was happening.

It was a garbage truck. Just like the picture book, only instead of bright green and cheerful and industrious, this one was hulking and dark and ominous.

And it appeared to be this Alpha's home.

CHAPTER 25

Hunter

Something was wrong. Very, very wrong.

Kess.

Hunter shot to his feet, sloshing his half-full glass of beer all over his hand and sleeve. Not that he had a moment's concern for that as he cleared the distance between the table and the back door through which his precious Omega had slipped. How long had it been? Five minutes? Six? He'd chatted with Mindy, aware of the trickling stream of anxiety rolling through his chest. Anxiety from Kess, venturing out into the world alone.

She'd been nervous about it. Even without the bond, he'd have known that from her uneasy expression. But the determined tilt to her chin and the steely straightening of her spine told him it had been important for her to try navigating this small part of the world on her own. The stubborn Omega valued independence, and using the John seemed low-risk enough…

You stupid fucking asshole. You let her go alone.

Hunt plowed through the restaurant, shoving and elbowing the mostly Beta crowd. He caught a few snarls from fellow Alphas, but nothing escalated, and he wasn't waiting around to see. Not while his Omega needed him.

Crashing out the back door into the murky gloom of the alleyway, the street chilled with baited silence. Latrine

207

doors hung open on their hinges, empty. No sign of Kess or anyone else.

"Kess!" he bellowed. "Kess!"

Only his own echo answered him. That and the dull thud of percussion from the bar band that throbbed against his temples like a gun to the head. Breathing deep, an assaultive array of smells flooded his keen nose. Kess was there, he could smell her panicked fear, along with dozens of others, including other Alphas. He sniffed again and again, running up and down the alley like a confused bloodhound, desperate to pick up a scent.

His Omega screamed inside him, her body calling to him, yanking on his chest, wild and so, so scared.

"Hold tight, baby," he muttered, his feet picking the route for him. He raced down alleys and lanes, doubled back, and switched up when the trail disappeared. Farther away from Mindy's and off the beaten path, he noted the twin odor wrapped around Kess' sweet Omega fragrance. A nasty, filthy Alpha smell that blinded him with pure, unadulterated rage. If the incident with Van had unhinged something inside of him, this was an absolute and total derailment.

Someone had taken his Omega.

And where *the fuck* were they going?

Angling around a corner at top speed, Hunt collided with another Alpha, striking him so hard they rebounded off each other in stuttering steps.

"Hey, what the fuck?" Before Hunt could catch his footing, another Alpha had ringed him round the neck and threw him against a wall. Two pairs of hands grabbed hold of his clothes and jostled him between them, jamming his cheek into the building and anchoring him immobile. "Why don't you watch where you're going, asshole?"

The Alpha's breath stung his face with paint-peeling alcohol content. Just great. His fucking luck to run into some drunk Alphas wandering a back alley. A cramping pain shot down his back as a third Alpha slammed a fist into his kidney. Hunt grunted, gritting his teeth.

"I'm looking for my Omega. She was taken," he pushed out, hoping he could end this altercation before it started. He could probably fight off three drunken Alphas with slowed reflexes, but it would take time he didn't have to spare. Every second that ticked by put his Omega further away from him and escalated the danger. He tried to appeal to reason, "I got no argument with you guys. Someone took my Omega, and I'm trying to get her back."

"Listen, old man, the only Omegas 'round here are at the whorehouse, and they're all worn out."

"Could hardly stand after we got through with them," the one behind him said to a round of stupid snickers. Three—there must be three.

Goddamn these fucking assholes. Terror screamed inside his chest. Terror and darkness. *Kess*. He felt it as acutely as he felt the second blow that landed on his other kidney. Kess was someplace dark, some secret place hidden from sight.

He needed to go.

Inside, his fury coiled, winding round and round like a tight spring.

"What's going on?" A fourth Alpha punctuated his question with the zip of his fly and the faint tang of watery piss in the air. "Who's this guy?"

Drunk asshole on the left answered, "Just some fucking geezer looking for a lost Omega."

"Here's what I'm saying." The drunk asshole on his right smirked in Hunt's face. "If you can't keep a handle on your Omega, maybe you don't deserve one."

"We passed an Omega being carried," the pissing Omega said with surprising sobriety. "She didn't look none too happy about it."

At this news, Hunt's barely leashed rage surged to the front, and he dropped his shoulder to shove off right-hand Alpha before driving an elbow into left-hand's face. The one behind him, who'd been happy to tenderize his internal organs the moment before, tripped over himself to move out of the way.

Hunt stepped up to the least drunk one, his voice lethal, "Who has her, and where did they go?"

"Don't know who," the sober Alpha explained, holding a quelling palm to his brothers waiting in the wings to re-assert their bullshit on Hunt. His disgust at their behavior must've shown through his fury, as chagrin blanketed the reasonable one's face. "She was fighting him, but we didn't think…"

Losing his shit completely, Hunt grabbed the Alpha's shirtfront to snarl in his face. "You saw an Omega in trouble, and *you didn't help her*? Jesus Christ, what the fuck kind of Alphas are you assholes? Which way was she headed?"

The Alpha pointed toward the outskirts, where the electricity dimmed and the darkness limned the abandoned buildings like overgrown tombstones. Dropping his grip, Hunt took off at a sprint in the indicated direction.

"C'mon, we'll help," the sober one called after, and the whole stupid group fell in behind him. He didn't want or need their idiot presence, but he didn't have time to deal with it. Sober caught up to him. "The Alpha who had her, he wasn't too clean-looking, and his scent is—"

"Rancid," Hunt supplied, his legs pumping. No other smells touched his nose, just Kess' faint sweetness and the festering Alpha musk clinging to it. Wherever he was taking her, it was secluded and dangerous.

"I scent an Omega too. Mated. Is that yours?"

Hunt grunted an affirmation as they followed the trail down a decrepit street. Abandoned buildings and no streetlights, so gritty it could hardly be real, like a parody of an apocalypse set in a horror film. Why had humans ever tried to imagine the nightmare their world could become? A thousand years of speculation and they'd never conjured anything close to the devastation of ten random minutes in the AfterEnd. All the reasons he'd decided to leave this hellhole... till Kess had changed his mind. Hell, she'd changed everything. But if something happened to her...

His heart contracted so hard he almost fell. Christ, was that what a heart attack felt like? If something happened to her, he'd be lucky to have a heart attack. But that wouldn't happen. Instead, he'd condemn himself to spend the rest of his unnatural life in abject misery. His punishment for having something so perfect and letting it slip through his fingers.

They raced to the end of the street, tasting the air for the trail and found… nothing.

"I don't think she went this way," Sober said, drawing large breaths.

Hunt spun, searching in every direction with his eyes, his ears, his nose, his fucking heart.

"What're we doing, Cal?" one of the drunken Alphas complained. "Thought we were going to get drunk?"

"Shut the fuck up!" Hunt hissed, pointing a finger at Sober, whose name was apparently Cal. "Keep your idiot friends quiet. She's gotta be around here somewhere."

Hunt paced the street, following the scent where it was strongest, sweeping left, right, and everywhere for any hint of movement.

Kess, baby, where are you? Help me find you.

CHAPTER 26

Kess

The Alpha's fetid palm locked around her mouth so hard her teeth tore the insides of her lips. Blood from the nosebleed he'd given her trickled into her ear. Her hands, swiftly tied and secured behind her back, ached from the combined weight of her body and his while his hips and massive Alpha legs neutralized her lower body. Restrained and immobilized.

Once he'd released her in the emptied garbage truck, she'd tried making a run for it, screaming for Hunt at the top of her lungs. But he'd caught her easily, making quick work of securing her hands as she'd screamed and screamed, not stopping until his palm made contact with her face. Which was further proof this Alpha was not well in any sense. No Alpha she knew of would strike an Omega, no matter how infuriated he was. Even Brock had never crossed that line.

Some part of this Alpha recognized the taboo of what he'd done, and he'd thrown himself into a flurry of half-baked apologies. Yet his behavior degenerated further before her eyes, her struggle spurring him deeper into insanity. She could see almost see the thoughts rolling behind his eyes. Surely his Omega wouldn't fight and run from him, right?

Cowed, she'd shivered in fright while he'd struck a match and lit an oil lamp, transforming the cavern into a collection of harsh, frightening shadows rather than pure, looming dark. He'd raised the squealing gate and secured some sort of blanket over the covering to block the light. Old and rusted, the lever required Alpha strength, which was a fair enough deterrent for any curious Beta intruders, she supposed. Or an unlucky Omega caught in his trap.

Clearly he was used to hiding, and this was his bolt-hole. The inside reeked even more than he did, and a festering bucket of waste in the back corner polluted her nose. A pallet of filthy rags made up his bed, upon which she was now restrained and miserable.

Only one thought held her the tiniest bit together. Hunt was coming. Hunt was coming, of that she had no doubt. The phrase repeated and repeated in her mind, a frantic prayer, answered by the uptick of his aggression as he realized her disappearance. Somewhere behind her, he chased, but how long and how far away, or how close he would get before this Alpha did something truly awful, she didn't know. Her muscles ached from battling against him. Realizing her helplessness and need to conserve her remaining strength, she went suddenly limp.

"Now are you gonna shut up, or do I need to find something to stuff in this mouth?" the Alpha growled close to her face.

She shook her head, a mere twitch of movement, and all she could accomplish with his hand locking her in place. His head lifted, but the crazed glare in his eyes didn't change. She lacked the strength to fight a full-sized

Alpha, even an unhealthy one, which left her only words to stall until Hunt made his way to her. The bond in her chest blistered and cracked with the heat of Hunt's fury. Every minute he tracked closer, and, if she knew anything about him, he wouldn't stop until he found her. One way or another. She just hoped it would be before this Alpha did something truly insane. If she could just get him talking…

"Alpha," Kess panted, "where was your bite? If I'm your Omega, where did you place your claiming mark? You should check and make sure it's still there."

It was a risk. It was possible his Omega, whoever that unfortunate soul was, wore his mark in the same place Hunt put hers, but on the off chance it wasn't, maybe that would get through to him. Even if it was in the same place, she wore a half-dozen other bites from Brock that she gambled no other Omega did.

"Don't you remember, Ava?" he said, giving her hair an awkward pet. "I never got to mark you. They took you from me, but here you are… you came back. I knew you'd come back to me."

A sad, wistful expression crossed his dirty face. *Shit*. If she directed him to her marks, there was no telling how he'd react to her scarred skin.

"*Shh!*" he hissed, his hand covered her mouth, his body stilling as he listened. Nothing moved in the garbage truck, nothing except the faint flickering of the lamp and the pounding of her heart.

Voices. Voices in the street outside. Deep, rumbling Alpha voices, angry and agitated.

Hunter. Her chest sparkled with recognition.

With her last bit of foolhardy strength, Kess thrashed under the Alpha's grip, wailing into his hand at the top of her lungs and attempting to kick out her feet and buck her hips. He'd been as heavy and immoveable as a boulder on top of her, but as he was caught off-guard by her sudden burst of activity, she twisted her hip to wiggle free a leg.

"Hunter! Hunter!" Her muffled screams were unrecognizable, but in her mad flailing, she kicked the side of the garbage truck with her freed foot. Pain lanced through her as she jarred her injured ankle, but she didn't care. The resounding, metallic *bong* filled her with hope. Hunt would hear it. He *had* to hear it.

"Shut up!" the Alpha seethed, his eyes wide and flying to the gate where the lever scraped open. The grating noise the sweetest she'd ever heard.

"Kess!" Hunter yelled.

No, his voice was the best thing she'd ever heard.

But it was quickly drowned out by commotion and shouts and Alpha smells as Hunter ripped the Alpha off her body and threw him outside the truck. One minute he was on top of her, and the next his body sailed through the gaping, monstrous jaws of the truck gate and was swallowed by the dark.

"Hold him!" Hunt ordered as the Alpha's body slammed into the ground with a muffled grunt. Hunt knelt at her side, pulling her up to free her hands. "Oh fuck, Kess, baby. I'm so sorry, I'm so sorry."

He muttered and fussed, a continuous stream of apologies as his hands raced over her body, checking her for injuries. His anger flared as he caught sight of her bleeding, swollen nose, but she threw herself against him before he had a chance to react.

"I'm okay," she breathed into his solid chest, drawing huge gulps of his just-right scent into her bloodstream. Her arms stretched around his solid torso, and she held on so tight, her tired muscles quivered. Not that she was letting go. She'd live the rest of her life attached to him like this, like a baby koala she'd seen in a book. "I knew you'd come."

"'Course I came." His harsh tone soothed her ragged nerves. She understood him now, enough to understand that this gruffness was not from his usual irritation or exasperation, but evidence of emotion too strong for words.

Long minutes passed as they held each other in the dank belly of an extinct machine. And slowly, slowly Kess' heart resumed a steady, peaceful rhythm.

"He kept calling me Ava," she said into his chest, her voice steadier. "He thinks I'm someone else, his lost Omega or something, I don't know... He wouldn't listen to me. Something is wrong with him, Hunt."

"He'll have more wrong before I'm through." Unwinding her arms, Hunt stroked a thumb down the side of her cheek to cup her face. His pale eyes, so piercing and beautiful, simmered with regret and adoration. "I'm so sorry, baby. I swear to you, I'll never let you down like this again, I swear it, Kess."

Her own hand rose to touch his beard, the thick texture alternately soft and bristly as her fingertips stroked with and against the grain. She basked in the heat of his gaze, the pure and utter devotion he shone down on her. He didn't want her for breeding pups or status or whatever instinct-driven reason Alphas and Omegas sought each other. He didn't speak to her Omega nature. He didn't speak to reclaiming her as a piece of property the other Alpha stole. He spoke to her. To his commitment to her. To the connection between them. *I swear it, Kess*, he'd said, her name like a benediction on his lips.

And she believed him.

His jaw hardened. "I'm never letting you out of my sight ever again."

She believed that too. The corner of her lip ticked up. "'Ever' is a very long time, Hunt."

The lines around his eyes creased in his version of a smile. "I'm counting on it."

With a tuck of his chin and a lift of hers, he kissed her.

CHAPTER 27

Hunter

Kess was safe, albeit a bit worse for the wear with her bloody nose and her swollen ankle. How long had she been missing? Fifteen minutes? Twenty? Hardly any time at all, and that piece of shit Alpha had her banged up and limping. One glance at her puffy, bloody nose was enough to rocket his anger back to lethal levels.

Secured in his arms, Hunt removed her from the stinking truck. The only thing he wanted was to spirit her back to Mindy's for a bath and food and every kind of pampering he could manage. But first, he had a rogue Alpha to deal with.

Outside, Cal and one of his friends held the stinking Alpha. The sight of the dirtbag boiled his blood, melting away the good feelings from holding Kess again.

It turned his stomach to let her go so soon after having her back, and his arms cramped in their own rebellious protest. "Stay here. I'm sorry you have to see this, but there's something I gotta take care of," he whispered as he eased her body down to a patch of grass.

She fisted a handful of his shirt, her eyes wide and imploring. "Be careful. He's not… a normal Alpha."

Her concern, pure and genuine, steeled his resolve. This monster had harmed his sweet, caring Omega, and he needed to die.

"Get the lamp," Hunt directed one of the onlookers. He wanted to get a good look at this degenerate. Even in the low light, his Alpha eyes noted they'd already roughed him up a bit. Not that he minded so much, as long as he passed final judgement. He wasn't keen on subjecting Kess to more witnessed violence, but frankly, he didn't see a choice. He'd pounded his own Pack brother to a pulp for a lesser insult. And that was when she'd been unclaimed.

Snatching another Alpha's mated Omega went beyond all instinct and natural law. True, there were no laws in the AfterEnd, yet society had reorganized around certain codes and conventions. Different in some ways for each dynamic, but ingrained and, per his estimation, baked into the genetic code. He'd no sooner attempt an abduction of a mated, bonded Omega than he'd cut off his own cock. The very idea made him recoil on a physical level, as if he'd brought a piece of rotten, maggoty meat to his lips.

Hunt stalked over, the restrained Alpha's wretched scent singing his nose. Could he not scent himself? With his large Alpha body and his overgrown hair and beard, he resembled the mythical Sasquatch said to stalk the Northwest before TheEnd. Light from the retrieved lamp approached and lit the stranger's face in detail. Seeping sores dotted the skin not obscured by dirty hair and beard, and a cut on his brow trickled fresh blood down a dirty cheek. In his hundred years in the AfterEnd, he'd never seen such an unkempt mess of an Alpha.

Kess was right; something was wrong.

Hunt studied his face, not through a lens of rage, but with a clinical eye, looking for an explanation that made sense given everything he'd observed about Alphas since his own transformation. Lamplight tracked upward, and the Alpha's bloodshot eyes held a fevered glow in their gray depths. The color gave him pause. Like his own, light-colored eyes were rare in the AfterEnd, as were lighter skin tones. Even concealed by dirt and sun-burnished, this Alpha had a pale complexion and dirty blond hair that worked itself into loose curls despite its filth. In fact, there was something oddly... *familiar* about this face.

At once, his body seized up like he'd collided with an invisible wall.

A ghost. He was looking at a ghost.

"Jake?"

The Alpha's eyes lit with a mirrored expression of shock, disbelief, and... recognition. He lurched forward, only to be yanked roughly back.

"Paul? Is that really you?"

Hunt's name, unused for so long, rocked him backward on his heels. Emotion rose up and sealed his tongue to the roof of his mouth. He could only stupidly nod his head, not wanting to take his eyes off his friend lest he disappear again.

His friend. He could see, beneath Jake's Alpha-sharpened features, remnants of his goofy friend with his floppy surfer hair and quick, easy smile.

Jake was alive! And here! And an Alpha!

And he'd stolen Kess.

"Hunt?" As if she'd heard his thoughts, Kess' scuffling, limping footsteps shook him awake. Her ankle obviously hurting, one of the Alphas offered her an arm.

"Don't touch her!" Hunt snapped, clearing the distance in two steps to support her side. Hunt drew her close, breathing in her comforting scent like a drug. "I told you to wait on the grass."

Her eyes flicked between Jake and himself, worry pleating her pretty brow. "You know him?"

"Holy shit, Paul! It is you!" Jake burst out, his energy hyping up to where he practically bounced between his captors. "This is crazy! What the fuck, dude?"

The phrase broke Hunt's inertia. *What the fuck, dude?* Jake had said it to him innumerable times during their friendship. It was so typically his old friend, goosebumps raised on his arms.

Stepping closer, with Kess' reassuring weight at his side, he stood at arm's length from his friend. They were of a comparable height, yet their powerful Alpha bodies so different from what they once were. And yet oddly the same. He imagined he appeared similarly to his friend.

Friend. The word scalded him with all its implied loyalty and obligations. His friend, whom he'd left in Mexico to see what remained of his family. Hunt couldn't regret searching for his family, even if the trip had only brought misery and no resolution. But he'd also promised Jake he'd return to Mexico so they could reunite, and he hadn't. Not when the full extent TheEnd's destruction—the bombs and radiation and disease and famine and plague—continued to unfold for months and years. Survivors dubbed it "TheEnd" because no one believed humanity would actually survive. And in many ways, they were right.

He'd justified not returning to Mexico, assuming Jake was either dead or had long since departed as well. But what if he hadn't? What if there'd been a window where Hunt could've helped his friend veer from this fate as a disgusting golem living in a cleaned-out garbage truck?

But none of that mattered. He'd hurt Kess. Hunt cleared the clog in his throat with a harsh cough. "You took my Omega, Jake."

Jake's chin jerked backward, his eyes blinking, blinking, blinking as they skittered between Hunt and Kess, widening into a manic gleam as he focused in on Kess. His mouth fell open as if remembering the events of the last thirty minutes.

"By rights, I'll kill you for that. What were you thinking?" Hunt's breaths shortened, shallowed by the tightness in his chest. "Can't you tell from her scent? She's *mated*."

Jake's head fell forward and hung on his Alpha-scrawny neck, a sign of defeat, deference, and submission. Yet it pacified Hunt none at all, and a cold chill ran down his neck.

He'd have to kill his friend.

Enraged at the indignity and injustice of it all, Hunt snatched a handful of Jake's shirtfront and pulled them nose to nose. "What happened to you? Why are you like this?"

Jakes face folded into one of absolute despair and shame. Hunt threw him back into the other two Alphas' clutches.

"I don't know. So many things. Too many things. I thought she was my Ava—" His voice broke, and he swallowed thickly, his eyes focused on Kess. "I'm sorry. I'm so sorry. It was the scratch…"

"Scratch?" Kess asked.

"A new drug finding its way into O.T.," Cal explained. "Strong. Unpredictable. Bad news." He cast another critical look at Jake. "Although I suspect that isn't the only thing wrong with this one." He turned toward Hunt. "What do you want to do, Alpha?"

A maelstrom of torment invaded his head, his chest, his heart. Jake had hurt Kess. Therefore, Jake needed to die. But he'd abandoned Jake all those years ago. Abandoned Jake and made a home for himself in the Canadian wilderness, where he was Alpha of Alphas. With a home and a Pack and, miracle of miracles, a kind, compassionate Omega at his side. An Omega he'd already killed for once. And would do again, without hesitation, if necessary.

But… was this necessary?

A gentle caress stroked down his back from shoulder to waist. Kess. Reminding him of her presence and lending her quiet support. He knew without asking that she wouldn't seek vengeance.

Her sweet, gentle heart and her strong spirit were too good for him. Her generosity and compassion were her strength. And with it, she'd survived. Survived to find her way into his arms, his bed, his life. He didn't deserve her, but he owed her. Everything he could give her and more.

Hunt closed his eyes, filled his massive Alpha lungs, and exhaled a long, long breath. When he opened them again, Paul Jason Hunter, the man-turned-Alpha who'd lived too long and lost his compassion and any trace of his empathy, allowed himself to ache for this pathetic remnant of his friend. He brushed the backs of his fingers down Kess' cheek, her face shadowed, but her beauty luminous.

He wanted to be done with this so he could be alone with his Omega.

He caught Jake's eyes, unleashing all his intensity and ire. "Here's how it's going to go." He spoke low and slow, his voice lethal and deadly fucking serious. There would be no room for equivocation or confusion. "Tomorrow, you're going to get yourself cleaned up. Wash, shave, find some clothes that don't smell like shit. My Second, Colt, is gonna come back here and bring you to my Pack. You'll fight your way in, like everyone, but I suspect you can take a beating as good as anyone. And when we leave O.T., you're coming with us. No more scratch, no more filth, no more Omegas. You don't touch an Omega, you don't *look* at an Omega. Fuck, I don't even want you to *breathe* near an Omega, you got me? If I see you near an Omega, I'll cut off your balls myself."

Jake's eyes widened in shock or fear or disbelief, but Hunt had no patience for questions or clarifications. He meant what he said. If Jake decided to push the limits otherwise, he'd find out how wrong that choice had been. "This is your choice. Fight me now, and I swear on my dead sister, I'll kill you without a second thought. Or you clean yourself up, join my Pack, and leave this fucking filth behind. And if you run, death will be the best you can hope for. Friend or no friend, we won't be having this conversation again."

Cowed and mute, Jake nodded, his eyes swinging to the Alphas gripping his arms and standing behind Hunt as if promising them as well. Returning his gaze to Hunt's, he nodded again, and Hunt saw the spark of comprehension, and maybe relief, in Jake's sad, tired eyes.

With a final, dismissive grunt, Hunter scooped Kess under her knees. "C'mon, baby. Let's get out of here."

"Alpha," Cal said as Hunt stepped past. Hunt kept walking. He could talk until he got to Mindy's, and then he didn't want to see anyone's face but Kess' for the next twelve hours. "Could we…" Hunt cut him a side-eye as Cal ruffled a hand through his hair. Not much more than a pup, Hunt realized, giving the kid a proper once-over. "Could we… uh… Are you taking on any more Pack members?"

Hunt snorted and nuzzled Kess' sweet-smelling neck. He licked her soft skin and nibbled on her dainty, precious earlobe, earning him a low, throaty laugh that shot right to his groin. Christ, why wouldn't they leave him the fuck alone? He picked up his pace, nearly at a jog backtracking his path to Mindy's.

"You want in, talk to Colt and fight your way in, just like that piece of shit back there. And,"—with annoyance, Hunt tore his eyes away from Kess to spear the young Alpha with a stare—"I ever hear you or your stupid friends disrespecting Omegas again, whores or not, you'll answer to me."

"Yes, Alpha," Cal said, glancing nervously at said idiot friends, who'd fallen into step behind them.

"Now get the fuck away from me," Hunt growled. "I've got an Omega to take care of."

CHAPTER 28

Kess

In her entire life, she'd never experienced the bliss of a warm, luxurious bath. Her dismay at this deprivation was offset by the added pleasure of being introduced to it by her mate. A thorough introduction, Hunter washed and scrubbed and generally fussed over her from head to toe. She could do little else but soak, a bemused smile percolating as he tutted around the bathroom.

Stalking the streets back toward Mindy's, his muscles had twisted with pent-up aggression. He'd forgone tearing Jake apart, as he no doubt planned, but his fight-primed physiology persisted far longer than the trip back across town. Only after he'd implored/menaced the bathhouse owner and busied himself hauling buckets of heated water to the free-standing tub did he start to uncoil. But now she was washed and refreshed, and Hunt had yet to sit down.

"Why don't you get in and have a turn, Hunt?"

"I'm just getting something for your hair," he grumbled, sorting through a stack of worn but clean-looking towels. "I don't want you to get cold."

"I'm sitting in hot water."

"Yes," he explained as if talking to a child, "but when we're done, you'll have to go back outside, and I don't want you to get chilled."

"I'll be fine." A muffled humph was her only response to this, so she changed tactics. "I thought you would keep me warm."

He pitched a look over his shoulder, his eyebrow cocked and a smoldering ember glowing in his blue eye. Good, at least he was settling down after the events of the night.

He handed her a small towel, and she gently dabbed her soggy curls. "There's probably more hot water ready by now. I'll go fetch it."

Kess studied her pruney fingertips. "I think I'm finished, actually."

Before he could argue, she heaved herself from the tub and sluiced droplets from her arms, belly, and legs, then reached to Hunt for a body towel. His gaze, the ember stoked to a roaring conflagration, sprung goosebumps from her arms despite the heat and humidity of the room. A pulse of reciprocal interest issued from between her legs.

Without breaking eye contact, he peeled off his shirt and pants and climbed in the tub. His massive body threatened to spill the water over the edge. He cared not at all, scrubbing himself with harsh, efficient strokes, his feral eyes never wavering. Heat pooled in her belly, and the first stream of fresh slick leaked between her legs.

Nostrils flaring, his expression darkened further, and Kess found herself creeping backward as his massive body emerged from the water and prowled across the room. She'd never seen him like this, his damp sun-kissed skin, the hard planes and bulges of his muscles illuminated by the artificial light through the humid haze. Despite the civilized setting, he remained a wild thing, brutal and savage… and hers alone. Her legs quaked with anticipation as her feet tripped backward to get away from the obvious predator in the room.

With one final stride, Hunt backed her into a wall and cuffed her neck, just as he had in her hut, only a short lifetime ago. Then, she'd shaken with dread, fear and uncertainty for this Alpha and his Alpha intentions. Now she shook with failing restraint not to throw herself into his arms and claim him as much as he'd claimed her.

Leaning forward, he dragged his nose from the base of her throat, up and over his bite mark, and toward her ear. His scent invaded her nose, fresh and clean but nonetheless all him. Her fingertips danced along the furred contours of his abdomen, hooking around his sides to drawn him closer, desperate to have his full weight against her full body. He didn't resist, huffing a pleased grunt that morphed into a groan as their skin slid together. Her nipples, hardened and aching, mashed into his wiry chest hairs, and she arched her back under his hold, scraping them against him. The sensation both a relief and a tease, she grabbed a firmer hold of his waist and hitched a leg onto his hip, grinding against him in shameless, urgent appeal.

"Feeling greedy, Kess, baby?" His teeth tugged at her earlobe, making her pant and whine for a taste. Any taste. His lips, his tongue, his fingers, his cock. She wanted it all. To gorge herself and give and take and give and take until she couldn't give or take any more.

"I need you." Her voice, throaty and hoarse with desire, rumbled in her throat. Hips working to ease the demand, her slick spread and perfumed the air between them. "Please."

Hunt's thumb traced the angle of her jaw and chin, snagging her lower lip. His eyes studied her, a sweet tilt to his gorgeous mouth as she nipped and nibbled at his thumb, trying to suck it into her mouth for the smallest, most pathetic of tastes.

His eyes turned solemn. "Finding you… was like waking from a nightmare. I didn't know it, but all this time, I think I was waiting for you. And it was worth it. Every painful, lonely minute was worth it." He dipped his head for a kiss, his mouth sweet and delicious and oh-so-earnest as he purred, "I would've waited another hundred years for you, Kess."

Her breath shuddered out. "I love you, Hunt."

"Paul." He swallowed. "When it's just the two of us, can you call me Paul? It's my old name, and I want to hear it on your pretty lips."

His request stilled her, so poignant and pure and… *perfect*. She kissed him again, drunk on the heat and taste and feeling welling up inside her.

"I love you, *Paul*."

He trembled under her fingers and dipped his forehead to rest against hers. His breaths sawed in and out, as if overcome from climbing his own emotional mountain.

"And I love you, baby. So fucking much."

Raising her hands, she cupped his face and brought his mouth back to hers, sealing their proclamations with heat and breath and fire. Over and over, she drank from his lips, drunk on the woodsy salt of his skin.

With his hands round her waist, he swapped their position to brace his back against the wall and slide to the floor. Kess followed him down, her knees cradling his thighs as she rocked her soaking core against his hot, hard, and insistent length. They groaned in unison, driving each other on as the energy ripened into something both precious and precipitate. His hands were everywhere, steadying her hips and handling her breasts, bringing them to his mouth to suck and nibble.

Her urgency surged fast and sharp. Ready to stake her own claim, she sank deep on his cock. It glided through the river of slick all the way to the hilt, and she gasped at the immediate fullness. The rightness. Her head fell back between her shoulder blades, and Hunt's tongue lapped at her throat. He growled and guzzled, his unrestrained hunger for her apparent.

Like a crack in a dam bursting with the pent-up energy and power, everything inside of her accelerated. Hips rocking, rubbing, grinding, she wound her hands around his neck and laced them into the long strands of his hair as she took her pleasure. Every movement exquisite and thrilling as it built to the next and the next and the next.

"Fuck, you are so sexy." His hands flexed and held her tight, following her movements as she spiraled into oblivion. "Go ahead, baby, take what you need. Take what's yours."

Her fingers fisted his hairline tight, and he sucked in a breath, more from pleasure than pain. Her thighs tautened up through her hips and belly and lower back. All of it primed and ready and hanging in the brutal precipice between want and have.

She panted a breath, "You are mine."

"Only yours," he gritted out, thrusting up deeper. "And you're mine. Forever."

Her climax rippled out from their joining, rhythmic pulsations that shot lightning up her spine. She whimpered, no longer able to form words as he thrust up and up, plowing deeper and rougher and finding his own release as the bulbous knot swelled and locked them together. Their noises—flesh on flesh and grunts and cries and then deep, exhausted breaths—filled the small, echoey room.

Kess collapsed onto Hunt's slab of a shoulder, licking at a stray droplet. Water or sweat, it didn't matter. If it was a part of him, she wanted it.

"Thank you," she whispered between light kisses to his warm, fragrant skin. "Thank you for finding me."

His arms wound around her and hugged her body closer than even seemed possible. "Nothing would stop me coming for you."

"Not just today. At the village too. I was hiding from the world. And myself." She lifted her head, meeting his clear blue eyes. Hiding from Hunter was never an option, but a world existed far beyond what she'd known or could even imagine. Even this little room, with warmth and light and hot water, stirred her imaginings. Freed from the confines of Brock's rules and her own self-exile in the Beta village, Kess would embrace whatever unknowns lay before her. "I don't want to hide anymore."

"Then you won't."

His words, so simple yet definitive, were rife with certainty and reverence and conviction. She had no doubt they were true.

"What happens from here?"

Hunt shifted his leg under her bottom and rested his head against the wall. "We'll stay here a few days. Rest, sleep in a bed—"

"We're going to actually sleep?"

"Occasionally." An uncharacteristically goofy smile played on his lips. "Then round up the rest of my Pack, fetch Jake, and head on home to Morris Hill. I want to show you around, show you off."

Kess grinned. "I'd like that."

"Good." He nodded once. Curt and to the point, just like him. Her heart throbbed with affection. After a pause, Hunt's brows bunched and furrowed the space between. "You gonna be okay, though, with Jake being around? After what he did? I should've asked you first, I suppose…"

Kess gnawed her lip and searched her feelings. "I understand why you did what you did. He's your friend." She rocked her head side to side. "I'm not sure I like it, but I'm not afraid. You wouldn't have done it if he was a danger to me."

"Never."

"I know that…" She laced her fingers behind his neck. "I just hope everything works out. For him."

Hunt dusted his knuckles up and down her arms. "Don't worry, I got a plan for him. He'll be under close... surveillance."

The statement, with its implied menace, sparked an improbable laugh. Kess covered her mouth, shaking to hold her giggles in at her oh-so-serious mate.

Eyes sparkling, Hunt dug a thumb into her ribs. "What's so funny?" Kess shrieked at the tickle, helplessly trying to twist away even as she remained pinned by the still-turgid knot. "Hmm? What's so funny? You're not laughing at me, are you?"

"No!" Kess' sides heaved, aching with giggles. "Never!"

She loved his unwavering austerity. But she loved knowing she might be the only person lucky enough to witness rare peeks of his charm and playfulness even more.

A smug grin cracking across his face, Hunt ceased his tickling and zeroed in on her swaying breasts. He cupped them with his rough palms. A wandering thumb toyed with her nipple, hardening it despite the warmth flowing through her veins. Her giggles ceased, breath stuttering an exhale.

"Love the sound of your laugh, baby." His gaze shifted from amused to smoldering. "But since we're gonna be here a while yet"—he lowered his grin to her flesh—"let's see if I can make you scream some more."

Sucking one tortured tip deep into his mouth, he punctuated this promise with a firm pinch to the other.

"You can try," she said, already restless and squirming.

"Oh"—he paused, holding her gaze as he licked her with the flat of his tongue—"I'll do better than try."

THE END

THANKS FOR READING
BONUS EPILOGUE & A FREE BONUS STORY

Thank you for reading The Alpha's Salvation! If you'd like to see more of Kess and Hunter, sign up for my mailing list at www.marloweroy.com! You'll get extra content including a bonus epilogue describing their homecoming in Morris Hill, spicy original character art, and a free novella from the world of the AfterEnd.

If you enjoyed The Alpha's Salvation, please consider leaving a review wherever you go to browse for books. As an independent author, reviews are invaluable for helping more readers find my book.

Want to continue the adventures with the Morris Hill Pack? Read on for a preview of Jake's story in The Alpha's Resurrection.

Not quite ready for Jake's redemption? Check out The Alpha's Seduction. It's Cal's story as he integrates into the Morris Hill Pack and the feisty older Omega who wants nothing to do with him.

xo, Marlowe.

FREE STORY:
THE ALPHA'S REVELATION

Nothing fazes Samson—not banishment from his Alpha Pack, not fending for himself in the wilderness, not even an unlucky encounter with an angry bear that leaves him mangled and on the verge of death.

He resigns himself to the inevitable, but fate has other plans. An angel with soft hands and a delicate voice appears and takes him to her bed.

Not as her lover, but as her prisoner.

Now, naked and restrained, fate plays her final trick. To gain his freedom, Samson must do the impossible and convince his suspicious captor she's Omega — and must submit to him.

FREE download now!
www.Marloweroy.com

ACKNOWLEDGEMENTS

To Deena and Jennifer, thank you for beta reading and cheerleading. To Natalie, thank you for the acerbic critiques and the late-night Hangouts text flurries.

Thanks to Dawn for the feedback, encouragement, and helping me become a better writer one MRU at a time. I'm sorry I dragged you into the omegaverse (sorrynotsorry).

Thanks to Merel and the Reticent team for this incredible opportunity and thanks to the omegaverse authors community for welcoming me into our weird, dirty little corner of romance.

To Dr. R., thanks for laughing at my jokes for years, making an excited fist pump gesture when I told you I was writing, and for saying many times "I can't wait to read it." That said, please don't read this book, although if you got this far, you probably already have. Please don't tell me.

And a heartfelt thanks and forever love to my husband for his support, both for this project and every other thing I've done in my life since we met a million years ago. You're the best and I don't know where I'd be without you, baby. xo, M

ALSO BY MARLOWE ROY
THE ALPHA'S SEDUCTION

She thought the apocalypse took everything, but in a world dominated by ruthless Alphas, there's always more to lose.

Della lived through the horrors of TheEnd. Dodging danger and violence for years, she survived with only her indominable independence to protect her. After finding a fragile peace in Morris Hill, she keeps to herself and guards her patched-up heart.

But when a mysterious Alpha with a sexy twang and arrogant swagger upends her quiet existence, she must choose: submit to him, or risk losing everything... again.

Haunted by the failures that destroyed his Pack, Cal wanders in self-imposed purgatory.

When a chance encounter brings him to Morris Hill, he finds everything he's longed for, including an Omega that sings to his soul.

READ NOW ON AMAZON

ALSO BY MARLOWE ROY
THE ALPHA'S RESURRECTION

One chance to choose her Alpha.

Zorah's on a high-stakes mission: choose one of the Morris Hill Alphas to bond before summer ends. If she fails, she'll return home and accept whomever her controlling parents pick, including her oily cousin.

With a dozen handsome Alphas vying for her attention, her future is under control. Until fate blinds her to all but one. Anti-social, reclusive, with a violent history, he's lowest in the pack.

And he's her mate.

His fresh start came with a price.

Desperate for a new life, Jake joins the Morris Hill Pack with a promise to never speak to an Omega. A high price he gladly paid for a shot at redemption.

But when his new village includes an irresistible Omega, he fears his resolve will crumble. Too young, too sweet, and too good for an Alpha trainwreck like him, he vows to stay away.

Forbidden to have and impossible to ignore, her nature calls to his; a destined collision he can't avoid. Giving in risks his redemption, his place in the pack, and his very life.

But giving her up will tear them both apart.

READ NOW ON AMAZON